A Vial of Life

A Shade of Vampire, Book 21

Bella Forrest

Cover design inspired by Sarah Hansen, Okay Creations LLC
Formatting by Polgarus Studio

Also by Bella Forrest:

A SHADE OF VAMPIRE SERIES:

Derek & Sofia's story:

A Shade of Vampire (Book 1)
A Shade of Blood (Book 2)
A Castle of Sand (Book 3)
A Shadow of Light (Book 4)
A Blaze of Sun (Book 5)
A Gate of Night (Book 6)
A Break of Day (Book 7)

Rose & Caleb's story:

A Shade of Novak (Book 8)
A Bond of Blood (Book 9)
A Spell of Time (Book 10)
A Chase of Prey (Book 11)
A Shade of Doubt (Book 12)
A Turn of Tides (Book 13)
A Dawn of Strength (Book 14)
A Fall of Secrets (Book 15)
An End of Night (Book 16)

Ben & River's story:

A Wind of Change (Book 17)
A Trail of Echoes (Book 18)
A Soldier of Shadows (Book 19)
A Hero of Realms (Book 20)
A Vial of Life (Book 21)

A SHADE OF DRAGON:

A Shade of Dragon 1
A Shade of Dragon 2

A SHADE OF KIEV TRILOGY:

A Shade of Kiev 1
A Shade of Kiev 2
A Shade of Kiev 3

BEAUTIFUL MONSTER DUOLOGY:

Beautiful Monster 1
Beautiful Monster 2

For an updated list of Bella's books,
please visit www.bellaforrest.net

Contents

Prologue: Julie

Eighteen years. That was how long I'd been waiting for Benjamin Novak to show up at The Tavern.

It had all started when I'd lost my parents and four siblings to a fire. It had been a warm summer night. I'd decided to sleep in the neighboring farmer's barn to get relief from the heat. Had I not, I would've died too when our bungalow went up in flames. Although I'd been only fifteen at the time, with my whole life ahead of me, on many a day in the aftermath of their death, I'd wished that I had burned with them.

I had no immediate relatives who were willing or able to help me, and with all our belongings burned in the fire, the thin nightdress I wore was the only possession I had in the world. I didn't even have shoes.

Within the span of several hours I found myself without my family or a roof over my head, and facing the prospect of sleeping that night on the street.

The only thing I could think to do was find work as a maid. I was willing to do any cleaning work, no matter how menial or laborious, to put food in my stomach. But dressed as I was, I didn't even know who would employ me.

By some mercy, the family who owned the farm next door took pity on me and allowed me to stay with them. I offered to work for free in exchange for food and a room. And so a little room at the base of their farmhouse became my home for the next few months… until one night the eldest son of the farmer slipped into my room and tried to force himself on me.

I narrowly escaped by striking him with the lantern that hung near my bed, but then I found myself without a roof over my head yet again. I tried for the next three days to find another job in the nearest town, asking in shops, pubs, even private homes whether they could use some domestic work. Due to the state of me, people took me for a tramp and nobody would invite me in.

After three days without a meal and drinking the drabs of clean water that I managed to come across, I arrived outside a building I'd hoped to never enter. The town brothel. But if I didn't eat soon, I was going to pass out.

Even then, as I walked through the door into the narrow, dimly lit entrance room, I was afraid that they would reject me. But as it turned out, I never got far enough into talking with the lady behind the desk to receive a rejection from her. I'd begun to explain my predicament and what I was willing to give up in exchange for a bed and a meal when a man I hadn't noticed interrupted our conversation.

Turning around, I was taken aback to see that he was a white man. I'd grown up in a remote and rural part of China, and this was the first white man I'd ever seen in the flesh.

He was… beautiful. Tall, broad-shouldered, with skin as pale as ivory. He had intense dark brown eyes that almost matched the color of the thick hair that touched the sides of his chiseled face. As I gazed at him, I found myself short of breath.

He spoke my language and asked if he could have a private word with me outside. I couldn't tell from his accent where exactly he was from, but it sounded soothing and exotic. I agreed, not sure what else a girl in my position ought to do, and he took my arm, his skin bizarrely cold against mine. He led me outside and told me that this wasn't a place for a girl like myself. That I deserved better. He wanted to take me home with him, with the promise of a hot meal and a soft bed.

This man could've been the devil, but I didn't know what other kind of monsters I might meet during a stay in that dark, dingy building. I figured that it was better to go with the devil I knew—or at least had met—than the devil I didn't.

And so I agreed.

He pulled up his horse—a towering black steed—caught my waist and placed me upon it before climbing up himself. As the horse sped up, I clung to the man's chest, feeling taut muscles through his shirt beneath my fingers. As he rode with me away from the town, he asked me what my name was and told me his. Hans Manson. And those were the only words we exchanged as we traveled along a remote, winding road, further and further away from any signs of human settlement.

A wild forest came into view in the early hours of the morning and we embarked along a narrow path that wound through the dense mass of trees. As I felt close to fainting from hunger and the exhaustion of holding on to him, we arrived in a clearing in the midst of the forest and I found myself gazing up at a… castle. A castle I hadn't even known existed in these parts. It was strange to see such a type of building in China. It had wide turrets and was distinctly European in design.

Entering the building, he led me up a grand staircase. I

would never forget how nervous I felt walking up the steps with him. I was fully expecting him to take me straight to his bedroom, to have his way with me even before he fed me. But he didn't. He led me to a bedroom, but it held only a single bed. He told me that it would be mine so long as I wished to stay here. He left me alone so that I could take a shower and change into a set of clean clothes that were already laid out on the bed—a beautiful silk gown. Though it was too long for me, I was grateful for it all the same. Then I returned downstairs to find him waiting to greet me. He led me into a dining hall where there was a long wooden table, already topped with food. It was simple food—hot bean stew, rice, and warm flatbread—and it couldn't have tasted more delicious.

Over the days that followed, he still made no mention of my joining him in his bedroom, and I found myself wondering exactly what he wanted of me in exchange for my lodgings. I offered to do work around the building, but he declined with a slight smile, saying that he already had a maid who came to clean for him. Though he said, if I was agreeable, he would like to spend time with me. Time doing what, he didn't specify, though it became clear over the weeks that followed.

Hans was a lonely man who wanted company. We spent hours sitting and talking. He was most curious to know about my background, though, slowly, he also began to share his own past. He said he was from England, although he had Swedish roots, and that he was a widower, having lost his love many years ago. He said he took pleasure in having a female companion, and that my presence lightened his dark castle. I didn't know what type of work he did, if any. He was always cryptic about it, but whatever he did, he seemed to be a man with a lot on his mind. As for his coldness, I could only think that he had some kind of medical condition. Or maybe people from those parts of the world were just cold-blooded? I didn't know.

I was surprised by how much I began to relish the time we spent together. He took on the task of teaching me English and proved to be a patient, conscientious teacher. We spent evenings together poring over books in the sitting room and he always sat with me at the dining table at mealtimes, even though he never ate in my presence. He just watched, as though me spooning food into my mouth was somehow fascinating. I chalked it up to a cultural difference. After all, I had no idea how people in England behaved. Perhaps it was considered rude for a host to eat at the same time as his guest.

After weeks of staying with him, I began to feel less like a guest and more like a part of his life. And I didn't quite know when, or even how, but I found myself falling for him. Weeks turned into months. Months turned into years. After two years of living with Hans in his castle, I was in love with him. In all that time, he'd barely touched me even in a friendly manner, and by the time my seventeenth birthday came around, I found myself wishing that we could draw closer. Even as he sat next to me on the sofa, he always seemed so... distant. Unreachable.

I wanted more. Of him. Of us. I wanted to feel his cool hand rest on my thigh as we sat together in the library at night, reading and discussing literature. I wanted to know what his lips would feel like pressed against mine. I wanted to feel the strength of his arms wrapped around my waist. Hear the beat of his heart through his chest as I rested my head against him.

I had fallen deeply in love with Hans Manson, a man who was still very much an enigma to me.

One cold, wintry night—the night after my seventeenth birthday—as we sat in front of the fire, Hans reading to me from one of his favorite novels, I found myself gazing into his handsome face. I summoned the courage to finally unleash what I simply could not hold back any longer. I reached up and closed my hand around the top of the book. I pushed it downward. My heart pounded as his soulful brown eyes rose to mine. I still remembered to this day the slight frown that set in on his face, the way he said my name in question.

Even as my pulse raced, I leaned closer to him. Reaching

up, I touched his face and before I could have second thoughts, I closed the distance between our lips and kissed him. Slowly, hesitant. He tensed and didn't respond at first. Horror gripped me and I was about to pull away, afraid that I had overstepped the mark. But then his hands slid into my hair. When his lips responded to mine, kneading hungrily against them, I only fell deeper for him.

I clung to him as he reached around my body, stood up with me and set me on my feet. He continued tasting my lips while his hands ran down my back and explored the curve of my waist. I was sure that he would've ended that night with just a prolonged kiss. But I made it clear from my body language that I was ready to give him more. So much more.

And so, in two years, that was the first night I shared Hans' bed. I was a virgin, and my parents had sheltered me. I had no idea what to expect, or even how it all worked. Despite the muscles I felt rippling beneath his skin, Hans was gentle and patient with me. Waking up in his arms the next morning, our bare forms still entwined, I didn't remember ever feeling so happy in my life.

From the way he'd always kept his distance with me, I'd feared that perhaps all he ever wanted was a platonic relationship. I'd feared that perhaps, even despite the two years we'd spent together, he really didn't feel any more affection for me than he would a friend. But that night, as he'd made slow, passionate love to me, it couldn't have been clearer that he did. I still couldn't be sure that his emotions were as strong for me as mine were for him, but I couldn't doubt the devotion I'd seen in his eyes, the affection of his embrace.

I realized that all this time, he'd been holding himself back. Perhaps, being the consummate gentleman that he was, Hans had wanted me to make the first move all along. He'd known that I was at his mercy and he hadn't wanted me to feel obliged to accept his advance.

That morning as he held me close to him, he asked me if I'd like to move permanently into his room. And so began our love affair. I shared his bed every night for the next two months. If I had fallen for him before, I was lost in him now. Being the unworldly teenage girl that I was, he became my life. I doted on him, and on the odd occasion when he left the castle, I watched the hours go by in misery.

It felt like every moment I spent with him, every affection he freely lavished upon me, was healing my broken heart. My heart felt full in a way I'd never thought it could again after the loss of my family.

I could never forget one evening, Hans asked me what he was to me. I felt shy, and wasn't sure what to say at first. He was my world. My life. He owned everything that I had—the clothes on my back, the food that I ate. And I realized that I wouldn't want it any other way. I wanted to be his. His forever. I barely saw anyone from the outside world. And I didn't care. He'd become all that I needed, all that I wanted.

I'd expressed myself that evening in stumbling words, hoping that he would understand what I meant. From the look in his eyes, he did. He kissed my lips tenderly and held me closer. "Then stay with me," he'd whispered into my ear. "Be mine."

And so I did.

At least, until fate tore us apart.

It happened one Sunday evening, six months after I first moved into Hans' bedroom. Soon after the sun set, there was a knock at the door. Hans and I had been sitting together in the living room. I couldn't miss the way his face tensed up. In my years of living with him, the middle-aged maid had been his only visitor.

Hans told me to wait in the room while he went to see who it was. But as he left, I couldn't help but peer through the crack of the door.

Hans opened the front door, and I could just about see who was standing in front of him—a tall, slender Chinese woman with short-cropped hair. Strangely, her complexion was only slightly darker than Hans'. She wore a cloak draped around her shoulders, and two robed men stood behind her with their hoods pulled down so low over their faces, I could barely make out their features.

Never in my wildest dreams could I have imagined what happened next.

Hans whirled around, his eyes wide with panic as he caught sight of me peering around the door. "Run, Julie!" he hissed.

I barely had time to move before the woman and two men leapt forward and grabbed Hans. Wrestling him to the ground, the three strangers overpowered him. A crack pierced the air as one of the men forced Hans' head to one side and disjointed his neck. I screamed, my whole body shaking as I rushed forward. They'd broken his neck. They'd killed him.

Before I could reach them, the two men had already hauled Hans' body off the floor and raced out through the door. They moved with such speed, speed that I'd never witnessed before in man nor animal. They were almost a blur to me.

The woman, still standing by the doorway, set her focus on me even as the two men dashed off into the dark woods carrying my beloved.

"Y-You killed him!" I gasped.

She approached me and gripped the back of my neck. Her hands were so cold, like Hans'.

"And who are you exactly?" she asked.

"Who are *you?*" I screamed.

"Ah, it seems Hans found a lover to fill his lonely heart.

How sweet. Well, fear not. Your man is not dead, only paralyzed. Do you wish to be reunited with him?"

"Take me to him!" I breathed, barely daring to believe her words.

"Come with me," she said, sliding one hand down my arm and gripping it. I was expecting her to lead me out of the door, but instead she held the back of my neck. She bared her teeth, fangs protruding. Her head shot down to my neck and I barely had a chance to cry out before her fangs sank deep into my flesh.

I wasn't sure exactly what happened next. It was just a blur in my memory. Perhaps I even passed out from the shock. All I knew was that when I woke up, I was somewhere very different. Somewhere cold and damp. And my insides felt like someone had doused them in acid. They burned so badly, I was convinced I was dying. The next hours were spent in agony until finally, as I looked into the cracked mirror in one corner of the dingy chamber, I found myself staring back at a monster.

Either Satan had possessed me, or I'd gone mad.

The woman came back and informed me that I was now a vampire, just like herself. She handed me a pitcher of blood and told me to drink it—which I did without question, hungrily, despite its bitter taste. She told me that I'd been brought to a coven in a different part of China. The vampire led me out of the dark room and along a narrow corridor. We entered another room, where I found Hans sitting in one corner. Then the woman left me. Hans sprang up and, realizing what I'd become, he staggered back, a devastated look in his eyes.

All I could think about was the fact that Hans wasn't dead. That he was standing right in front of me. I threw myself at him, reveling in his embrace as he showered my face with kisses. I'd seen those people snap his neck, even heard the crack of bone. Yet here he was. He pulled me down on his bed and, cradling me in his arms, began to reveal his full history to me for the first time. Everything he'd been holding back since the day we'd met. He told me first that, indeed, there were such things as vampires. He was one, and now I was one too.

He told me that he and his wife had been turned almost two hundred years before, along with his four siblings. They'd all been taken to the coven where we were now, deep in the Taihang Mountains. His wife had been murdered by another vampire over a dispute while living there, and after he'd lost her, Hans couldn't bear to remain in the coven any longer. He and his siblings had tried to escape together, and while the latter had failed, Hans had managed to. He'd been in hiding ever since, in that old castle buried in the woods in the middle of nowhere, and he'd hoped that they would never find him.

He clutched my head in his hands, kissing me again and again even as he repeated how sorry he was, how he loved me and how dragging me into all of this was the last thing he'd wanted.

I told him that I didn't care, that I was just grateful that he was alive and that we were together. I told him that, vampire or not, I would follow him anywhere. Because I was his. He held my heart and every part of me.

We spent the next four decades of our lives together in that Chinese coven. Or as together as we could be. Sometimes we were forced to split up and travel with different groups on nighttime excursions. But we were given a small apartment where we could live together and during the day, for the most part, we had each other. The vampires promised Hans that if he attempted to escape again, they would track us down and stake me through the heart in front of his eyes. Even though I suggested that we try it, it was for my sake that he refused. They'd already managed to track him down once, and he wouldn't take the risk of that happening again.

Even in these circumstances, I couldn't complain about my life. Hans was the only thing that I needed to be happy.

The nights became our days, and the days our nights. We fell into a mindless routine during the night hours that consisted primarily of procuring fresh human blood and bringing it back to the coven. And during the day, Hans and I could bask in the fire of our love, still burning as strong as the night we'd shared our first kiss.

Then one day our lives were uprooted yet again. The same woman who'd turned me into a vampire all those years ago knocked on our door again. She didn't attack Hans this time as he opened the door, but the words she spoke caused Hans' face to pale as I'd never seen before.

She told him that we'd both been selected to be transported to Cruor. She promised that we would both be performing important and valuable service to our masters, the Elders. Masters I'd only heard vague talk of around the coven.

Hans fought against the idea, but in the end, we had no choice in the matter. We were taken to a portal and brought to the desolate red-tinged landscape that was Cruor. The land of the Elders.

We were taken into the bowels of a mountain, where layer upon layer of shadowy chambers had been built. It was there that I discovered the truth about those known as the original vampires. Hans and I had been brought there to be used primarily as vessels, to do their bidding in whatever task they had. The Elders would inhabit us and we would descend into the deepest depths of the mountains, where giant halls filled with pools of shimmering blood were kept. We would be forced to drink liters of it at a time, thus sustaining and bringing pleasure to the Elder who'd inhabited us during the feeding.

Still, even through all of this, Hans and I were granted a room to ourselves, which became our refuge from the Elders' ghastly abode. We lost track of time while living in that strange place. But I suspected that decades passed. Over time, our bodies became weaker. Although usually the Elders were careful to give us rest after being inhabited, sometimes they didn't, which left us feeling drained and unwell.

Then, eighteen years ago, the climate between the Hawks and the Elders changed irrevocably. Due to a spiral of incidents that had happened in the human realm, the malice that had been brewing between the two species reached the boiling point and our lives changed forever. The Hawks stormed Cruor, entering the Elders' mountain chambers, murdering vessels, and soiling all the blood supplies that we had collected for decades.

During the first wave of the Hawks' attack, Hans and I had been locked in our room. A Hawk broke down the door and barged into the room. With a combined effort, Hans and I managed to slit his throat before escaping through the door.

The halls outside belonged in a nightmare. Countless bodies of our fellow vessels were strewn about the floors as the giant birdlike Hawks tore through the halls. Hans and I had to escape the mountain—and go where exactly, we didn't know.

We had almost made it to the exit at the top, with just one last staircase to climb before we arrived out in the open, when Hans' hand jerked away from mine. I whirled around, afraid that a Hawk had just caught him within its talons. But no, Hans had torn his hand deliberately from mine. As I stared at him in confusion, the expression on his face made me realize what had happened. An Elder had entered him.

For reasons I couldn't understand, the Elder made Hans turn on his heel and run back into the chaos of the corridors. I cried out and raced after him, but a Hawk swooped down in front of me and I was forced to dive out of the way. After that, I lost sight of Hans. I had no idea where he'd gone. I searched the halls, corridors and chambers desperately, even despite the mortal danger I was putting myself into by weaving in and out of the battle.

But no matter how much I searched, I couldn't find Hans.

With more Hawks arriving by the moment, the place overflowing with the birds, I sought out a small cupboard at the bottom of the staircase and squeezed myself inside, closing the door and hoping that nobody would notice me in the heat of the battle. I'd be killed if I roamed around this place screaming out Hans' name. I had to wait for the battle to die down and for things to become less dangerous.

I had to wait in that tiny, cramped cupboard for days before the Hawks had drained the place of all vessels. When I finally stepped out of the cupboard, the wrecked chambers were deserted. I had no idea what had happened to the Elders. I raced around the corridors, tears stinging my eyes, as I searched once again for my love. Even though I knew it was hopeless—there was no way that he would be here—I had to find him. Even if it was just his body. I had to see him again.

But even his corpse I could not find. He'd disappeared without a trace. I spent the next few weeks wandering those bloody mountain chambers like a spirit. I felt bound to that place, the last place I'd seen Hans, hoping against hope that somehow he was still alive and if I only waited long enough... he'd return.

I lost myself in the darkest depths of depression. After weeks without blood, my stomach hurt as though it was starting to eat itself. Eventually, I was forced to leave in search of nourishment.

It was as I exited the mountain and began clambering over the rocks toward the shore that I sensed an Elder's presence. A voice, weak and strained, hissed in my ear. "We have your lover," he said.

His words were like an electric jolt to my chest. My mind, previously dulled with mourning, sprang to life.

"Where?" I gasped. "Take me to him!"

"You go too speedily, girl. During the Hawks' siege, we selected a number of vessels to hold back from the battle and keep safe. Hans was one of them. He is quite secure, within a secret chamber in Cruor that you will never find unless shown."

"Show me!" I said, my voice cracking. "Please, take me to him!"

"Certainly, you can see him again," the voice rasped. "But not until you fulfill your end of the bargain."

"I'll do anything. What do you want from me?"

"You must help us fulfill a prophecy," the voice hissed. I listened with bated breath, scared to even miss a word he said. "I and your other Elders have lost strength, too much strength, as a result of this battle. Even if we had pure human blood within reach, we could not gain sustenance from it sufficient for recovery, because we are too weak to inhabit these vessels… However, there is a hope for us. Basilius imprinted upon a certain human infant in anticipation of the battle. A human child with… unique blood. Unfortunately, he is now returned to earth, but his time will come to rise and help us. That much we know. The day his parents turn him into a vampire will be the day he starts his journey back to us. His name is Benjamin Novak. If you wish to see your lover again, you will play a part in helping him along this journey."

"When will he turn?" I stammered. "You said that he is just an infant now."

"Just short of eighteen human years from now, he will be

turned."

"H-How do you know that?"

" 'Tis the prophecy."

It felt as though someone had bored a hole in my stomach. "Eighteen years?" I breathed, winded. "I cannot wait that long. *Hans* cannot wait that long. How… How would he even survive without blood for all that time? You have no blood, and you are too weak to procure even animal blood, it seems. How will—"

"Silence." The voice sliced through my protests. "You have heard what your task is."

"Can I just see him?" I begged. "Please, just let me see him. I promise I will—"

"You have heard my terms, Julie Duan," the voice said, and then the chilling presence left me.

I sank to my knees on the sharp rocks. I breathed heavily, my mind working furiously as to where the Elder could possibly be keeping my love. Although I'd spent what felt like an age in this barren wasteland, I still didn't know it well. Hans and I were usually kept in our quarters in the mountain and we didn't often venture out except on the Elders' bidding.

In spite of my weak limbs screaming for blood, I spent the next three days roaming about the landscape, desperately trying to discover the hidden chamber. Being unsuccessful, I was forced to go to the shore and feed myself with the blood of sea animals before resuming my mission with more strength. I was so determined to find it, I searched for an entire month.

When I still didn't find him, I lost hope that I ever would. Indeed, as the Elder said, the chamber was hidden so well that I would never find it no matter how long I searched for it. And so, my heart weighed down by the Elder's prophecy, I left that island on a rickety boat I found abandoned on the shoreline. It had a tiny covering over it to keep the sun from burning too severely into my skin, and I set off, drifting out into the ocean.

Eighteen years. The word played over and over in my head like a nightmare. How could my love even be alive by then without blood? That was my foremost concern. Although eighteen years was a horrific amount of time for me to be away from my soulmate, we were, after all, vampires. Immortals. In the grand scheme of things, eighteen years was but a blip in time. And if I managed to free him then we could be reunited again. It was the thought of Hans starving that sent me into a panic. During my search of the mountains, I had screamed at the Elder countless times to at least allow me to bring blood for Hans. But the Elder never returned.

I had no choice but to pray to the heavens and hope that

somehow, Hans would survive.

I ended up reaching The Tavern and stayed there for a while. It was on that island that I happened to come across Hans' siblings. Unlike Hans and me, they hadn't been chosen to go to Cruor. They had remained in the coven in China, but since the Elders had been forced back through the gates, his siblings had been freed from the coven and found a gate leading into the supernatural realm, where they had become wanderers.

I told them everything that had happened to their brother and they shared in my devastation. As painful as my longing for Hans was, his siblings gave me strength. We stuck together from then on, trying to survive, keep each other safe as we waited for the years to pass. I returned to Cruor on a regular basis, clambering over rocks, just in case that human boy had turned into a vampire sooner and we could complete the task earlier. I was sure that the Elder would sense my presence and inform me. But even though I spent days at a time in that desolate land, giving the Elders ample opportunity to connect with me, none did. So I could only assume that eighteen years would indeed be the time that we all had to wait to see Hans again.

His siblings also had no idea how he was going to survive without blood, or if that was even possible for a vampire. We asked others also, but nobody seemed to know what truly happened to a vampire when they starved, how long they could survive, and if they ever died from starvation. I guessed that vampires never went that long without blood. They always found a way to get it somehow—by murdering either a human or animal.

And so we waited. And waited. Until finally, as the eighteenth year was on the cusp of arriving, while I paid my routine visit to Cruor, the same Elder spoke to me. I'd never thought that his frightening voice could be such a welcome sound, but relief washed over me as his hiss met my ears.

"You have been patient, girl," he said. "And soon you will be rewarded. The time has come. The human boy has been turned and is closer to reaching us now than ever before. Go and wait in The Tavern, and keep an eye out for him."

The Elder gave me a description of Benjamin Novak's physical appearance, and warned me that he was stronger than most vampires. He also told me that he was being accompanied by two jinn—creatures I had thought were merely a myth. Other than that, he didn't offer advice as to how I was going to pull this off. I guessed figuring this out was part of earning my right to see Hans again.

I hurried back toward the ship where Hans' siblings waited for me. We left Cruor and sped toward The Tavern. The only thing on my mind was Hans. How he had been keeping all these years. How it would feel to touch him once again.

Hans' siblings and I spent the following days in The Tavern. I figured that if Benjamin Novak arrived here, he was bound to visit the pub in the town square, since that was the central hub of this island. I decided that I would spend most of my time there. Hans' siblings positioned themselves in other strategic points to keep a lookout.

It was on one such occasion that Hans' youngest sibling—his sister, Arletta—spied two other members of our Chinese coven, brothers. They too had escaped and become wanderers in the supernatural dimension. Arletta reported that they were just passing through The Tavern, and she had overheard them speaking of a special box they had managed to steal from a warlock. It purportedly had the ability to contain ghouls and other subtle beings. I didn't know whether it was true, but my instinct told me that this box could be useful for the task ahead of me.

And so we plotted to steal it. I recalled that those brothers had harassed me once in the coven. Soon after Hans and I had arrived, they'd tried to make an approach. That was before they'd been aware that Hans was my lover. Now I figured I could use their attraction for me to my advantage. I caught the two alone near The Tavern's port one evening. Of course, they were shocked to see me at first, but I soon eased them into a conversation after explaining I'd split up with Hans. I seduced them into joining me for a walk along the beach, and in the meantime, Hans' three brothers stole the box from the brothers' ship and transferred it to ours.

I slipped away from them gracefully and returned to the pub where I sat facing the wall, looking back over the room every time the door opened.

That night, Benjamin Novak finally arrived. Since mine was the emptiest table, he headed straight for me and took a seat. My act had begun. I had to clutch my glass tight to stop my hands from trembling with anticipation. It felt like I'd waited an eternity for this young man. I didn't know anything about him yet, but I did know that in order for me to bring him back to Cruor, I needed to be smart. The Elder had said that he was protected by jinn—and I didn't know much about the creatures other than they were to be feared. I figured that the easiest way to gain his trust would be to begin by offering him casual, unconditional help, and later, make myself out to be a victim.

Two happy coincidences came along that very night.

First was the presence of humans in the guesthouse—not just the cleaner downstairs but also another apparently staying in one of the rooms near Benjamin's—which forced Benjamin to come upstairs. And second was the two brothers smashing through my window. I'd known they'd be angered when they realized the box was missing and they'd probably suspect I had something to do with it—but I'd never dreamed that they would attempt to murder me for it.

This incident brought Benjamin to me yet again, and this time in a much more permanent way. I had an excuse to insist that we both leave the island immediately. I'd considered suggesting from the start that we travel together, but that might be coming on too strong. He would wonder why I couldn't just travel in my own boat. So, as we arrived in the harbor, I stopped at a random boat and told Benjamin it was mine. Then I had a few moments to destroy the boat, leap into the ocean and slaughter the sea creatures. I'd worried he'd think it odd that my clothes were drenched, but I'd figured by now that Benjamin was a gentleman and probably wouldn't pay much attention to it when he saw me "stranded" and calling for help. And that was exactly how it played out as he raced away with me on the boat he'd stolen.

After that, slowly but surely, I worked toward getting to know him and building myself up as someone he could confide in. When we went to meet with Arron for the first time, Benjamin revealed the level of trust he already held for me by defending me from the jinni who intended to kill me for my heart. I sensed the incident was a pivotal moment. From then on, I just had to keep sowing the seeds of my loyalty and concern for his well-being… all the while trying to figure out how the hell I was going to put a wrench in the works of this surgery Arron had suggested, get rid of the jinn's protection over him, and deliver him safely back to Cruor.

It was a frighteningly epic feat ahead of me, and to make matters more difficult, I wasn't a scheming person by nature. I considered myself honest and straightforward. But desperation did things to people. When a person had enough on the line, they could accomplish anything. I had to hope that if I stayed with Benjamin long enough and managed to prevent the surgery, sooner or later I would get him on his own, without a jinni protecting him. Although I had no idea how, and I certainly hadn't expected that it would happen in such a smooth manner.

When we returned to the witch physician Uma's island with the ingredients and Benjamin found out that the merflor was missing, he immediately suspected Arron—although, of course, it had been me who had removed and destroyed it. Then a few moments later as we stood on that hilltop discussing returning to The Cove to collect more merflor, Bahir vanished. That left only the jinni inside Benjamin to deal with. I knew then that I had a good chance of luring him back to our ship with the idea of the Elder box.

Then the Hawk practically took himself out. I'd suspected from the look in Arron's eyes that he was planning to attack Benjamin. But I waited until he neared Benjamin with the iron bar before leaping at him and tearing out his throat—I had to do it while Benjamin was watching, so that he could see how I'd saved him yet again.

After that, Benjamin Novak had no more options. There was nothing left that he could do but take my suggestion to come with me to retrieve the box.

As soon as we reached the ship and I brought him on board, it was plain sailing. Since he'd been so unsuspecting, we had the element of surprise on our side and it wasn't long before we'd locked him in the box.

Now he was with Basilius. As I and Hans' siblings moved down the mountain to meet with the Elder who had promised to finally take us to see Hans, I thought of Benjamin Novak, lying paralyzed on that cliffside. Perhaps his Elder had already taken him over by now.

It had been hard to remain stoic throughout my betrayal. I hadn't wanted to do what I did to Benjamin. The more I'd gotten to know the vampire, the more difficult the task had become because... he was a good man. I didn't want to cause harm to him and yet delivering him to the Elder was the only way I could see Hans again. My yearning for my lover blinded me to all else and almost numbed me to the guilt.

Once we reached the foot of the mountain, I shoved aside thoughts of Benjamin. We'd arrived outside an old oak door etched into the mountain wall—one I recognized too well.

My breathing became harsh and erratic. *This is it. Finally, the day has come.* I exchanged glances with Arletta, who stood next to me with clenched fists.

I stepped forward and knocked on the door. "We brought the boy safely to Cruor," I called. "Now he is with Basilius."

I sighed with relief as a cold presence closed in around us. The door creaked open and we stepped inside a long dark tunnel.

"Straight ahead," a voice hissed.

I was surprised that we were going along this route. It was one of the main entrances to the Elders' mountain abode. *Could they really be keeping Hans and the other vessels here?*

The path wound deeper and deeper into the mountain until the Elder commanded us to stop. Strangely, it was right in the middle of the tunnel. There were no doors or anything nearby… at least not that I could see.

Then Arletta pointed to our right. A ridge ran down the wall from top to bottom to form a perfect ninety-degree angle.

"Enter through this door," the Elder commanded.

No wonder the Elder had said I would never find the place where Hans was hidden. When passing through long tunnels like this, one didn't pay attention to the walls. They faded into the background.

Arletta and I pushed against the stone with all our strength, but it was incredibly stiff. As though it hadn't been opened since the day it was locked.… Perhaps even eighteen years ago. Fear filled me. *Will Hans really not have consumed blood for eighteen years?* Although I didn't see how he would have been able to consume it since the Elders weren't supplying it, at the back of my mind I'd held out hope that somehow he'd managed to procure enough blood to stay healthy. *Please be alive. Please be alive.* I repeated the mantra over and over in my head like a prayer.

Hans' brothers helped out with the stone entrance and, with all of us pushing at once, the door ground open.

Before us was another long, dark tunnel, the ground and ceiling cluttered with stalagmites and stalactites. We had to watch our step to avoid being gouged. After five minutes, we reached a dead end.

"Now what?" I murmured.

"This is another door," Braithe, Hans' second youngest brother, said. And he was right. Before us was the same ridge. Again, it required all five of us to force it open. The grating of stone against stone sent echoes bouncing around the walls, making the place feel all the more eerie. We stepped through the second door and arrived at the top of a jagged stone staircase—at the bottom of which we could spot yet another door, this one locked with a bolt. I wondered how many more doors we'd have to pass through.

We reached the bottom of the staircase and, drawing aside the thick metal bolt, began to tug on the third door. Just as it felt like we were on the verge of prying it open, the Elder spoke again.

"Beyond this door, you will be reunited with the vessel you seek."

As Hans's siblings continued to tackle the entrance, I drew away and held up a hand. "Wait," I whispered. Now that we were on the precipice of seeing Hans again, fear washed over me—fear of what we might see behind this door. Most of all, I feared seeing his wasted corpse.

Hans' siblings respected my wish to take a few moments to steel myself before barging through the door. I was sure that they were taking the opportunity to do the same. Sensing that the Elder's presence was still with us, I asked him in a shaking voice, "Is Hans actually alive?"

There was a pause. An agonizingly long pause. Then the Elder gave me the least comforting answer he possibly could. "I know not," he whispered back.

My mouth dried out. "How can you not know?"

"Neither I nor any of my fellow Elders have entered the chamber since we locked them in here for safekeeping almost two decades ago."

Safekeeping. They wanted to keep these vessels safe. The Elders must have been convinced that they would survive. Otherwise what was the point in locking them in here? They might as well have just let them perish like their other vessels.

Still, I couldn't keep myself from asking, "Do you really not know what happens to a vampire when they starve?"

"I do not know," the Elder responded, a hint of impatience in his tone. "I have never witnessed the result of starvation in a vampire before. Open the door and we shall see...."

As we resumed our hold on the door and forced it loose, we geared ourselves up to likely be the first people in history to find out.

***

Nothing could have prepared me for the sight that lay beyond that stone door.

As we stepped through into a pitch-black dungeon—darker than even the dank corridors we'd been traveling along— the first thing that hit me was the smell. The thick stone walls had contained and stifled it while we had been standing on the other side, but now it was unbearable.

The scent alone sent my mind into a panic. Vampires indeed could starve and the smell was that of rotting corpses.

But the strange thing was, as I cast my eyes despairingly around the large, circular chamber, there wasn't a body to be seen. The floors were empty, except for the odd puddle of water.

"The ceiling!" Braithe choked.

As my eyes drifted upward, I stopped breathing. The

stalactite-ridden ceiling was lined with… bodies. Naked, stark-white bodies. I stumbled further into the chamber, my head hanging back as I gazed upward in disbelief. The bodies… they were utterly emaciated, their skin—if it could even be called that anymore—was thin as papyrus. From where I stood, I could only see their backs, but I could see the backs of their heads—each devoid of even a strand of hair.

No. This isn't happening. This isn't happening.

"Hans!" I croaked. My cry echoed around the chamber, causing it to sound all the more anguished.

I staggered into the center of the room, falling to my knees as I continued gazing up hopelessly. Were they dead? How were they all clinging to the ceiling like that with their hands and feet? They all appeared motionless.

Almost as soon as I had the thought, the last of the echoes of my cry fading in the room, they began to stir. The sound of cracking filled my ears—cracking bone. They loosened their tight hold on the uneven ceiling and the next thing I knew, their legs dropped loosely beneath them. Now their faces were no longer obscured, I was able to witness the full horror of their transformation.

Oh, God.

What have they become?

Their faces were shrunken, as were their lips, and their noses had receded into their skulls. Their eyes, small black dots in the center of their eye sockets, stared down at me, unblinking. I scanned the ceiling to see if I could recognize Hans. They were all so horrifically transformed.

"Hans," I called weakly.

Please let this be a nightmare. Please. Don't let Hans be lost to me.

Arletta clutched my hand as the body—a male—hanging directly above us shifted. We all stood back as his hands detached from the ceiling. He dropped to the floor and crumpled in a heap. *Could this be him?* We rushed forward, and I reached out, my insides squirming as I touched his papery, skeletal shoulder. He seemed too weak to stand up. I gripped the upper portion of his bony arm, afraid that it might snap even at the slightest pressure. Braithe clutched his other arm and slowly, we raised him to his feet.

Now I was able to take him in fully for the first time. He was approximately the right height for Hans, allowing for the bend now in his spine. And although his face was so horribly deformed, I could just about make out the shadow of his familiar strong jawline.

"Hans?" I urged.

He stared back at me blankly.

"Is that you, brother?" Braithe asked.

He continued looking at us as though he either couldn't hear, or didn't understand.

What happened to you?

"We need to get him out of here," I choked, looking desperately at his siblings. "We need to get him back to the ship and feed him blood. He'll recover. I know he will."

Although my brain told me that he would never recover from such a state, my heart couldn't let go. I held onto the irrational hope that somehow, if we just fed him enough blood, he would recover slowly but surely, and he would be mine again. Hans. The same man I'd fallen in love with.

"Arletta, Julie." Hans' youngest brother, Colin, addressed us. "Go open the door wider so we can carry him through. I'm not sure he can even walk."

Although I didn't want to leave Hans' side, we did as Colin suggested. Arletta and I hurried back to the door and heaved it open wider, as wide as it would go.

A snarl came from behind us. Then a strangled yell. Braithe's yell.

Arletta and I whirled around to see Braithe on the floor, Hans on top of him… attacking his throat.

I was too stunned to even move. But Arletta shrieked and raced forward.

The siblings hauled Hans off Braithe, and as they pushed the former away and helped Braithe to his feet, I could see that Hans had ripped a huge gash in his neck. Braithe looked in agony as he gripped the side of his throat and attempted to stem the blood flow.

Sharp fangs still bared, Hans wiped the blood from his mouth with the back of his bony hand before his dull eyes fixed on me. More bodies dropped from the ceiling and stood to their feet. Their gazes narrowed in on us.

"We have to get out of here!" Braithe wheezed. He was already the slowest of all of us, his leg having not yet fully healed after Ben injured it. His brothers held his arms and dragged him toward me and the door.

I just stood, frozen. As Hans' siblings exited the room, I couldn't find my feet to follow. *Hans is still here. We have to take him with us.* Even as the emaciated vampires began lurching toward us with alarming speed—Hans at the forefront—a manic gleam in their tiny black eyes, I still stood there, stunned. If Colin hadn't grabbed my arm and forced me through the door, I would've stayed there. The brothers slammed the stone door closed after us and bolted it just as bodies hit up against the other side, scratching and clawing at the stone.

"They were all going to attack us," Arletta gasped, clutching her chest as she breathed out.

"Hans," I whispered, staring at the door. "He's still in there! We have to get him out."

Braithe, who sat on one of the stairs nursing his throat, shook his head, his face ashen. "Not until we figure out what the hell Hans has become."

"Elder? What was that?" Frederick, Hans' other younger brother, demanded.

The voice took a moment to reply. "Something… peculiar. Perhaps even… miraculous."

"Miraculous?" Arletta cried. "My brother, he—" She broke down sobbing on the floor. I would've joined her, had I still not been so shell shocked.

"During their starvation, it appears they reached a boundary from which there was no return," the Elder mused.

Before anyone could ask anything more of the Elder, Braithe let out a guttural roar of pain. It came so suddenly, my heart leapt into my throat and I jolted back in alarm.

Arletta scrambled up from where she'd been crumpled on the floor and gazed down at her brother, along with Frederick and Colin. Braithe slid from his seat on the stairs and tumbled to the ground. We were about to dip down and help him back up when claws protruded from his fingers and he lashed out, catching Colin's arm.

"Braithe?" Colin gasped, staring down at the gash his brother had just ripped in his arm. "What are you doing?"

Braithe let out another roar, so loud and so anguished that one would have thought he was being murdered.

"Elder, what's happening?" I asked, my voice trembling.

But the Elder's presence had slipped away.

"I have no idea what's wrong with our brother," Frederick said, straining to contain Braithe, "but we need to get back to the ship. Before we can help Hans, we've got to figure out why Braithe is reacting like this."

"But Hans is—" I began, weakly.

"Julie!" Colin snapped as he helped Frederick restrain Braithe, who was continuing to lash out. "Get a grip. Hans has been trapped in there for eighteen years. A few more hours, or even days, won't make a difference while we gather together some blood for him so he doesn't try to attack one of us again, and try to figure out what in heaven's name is going on."

Frederick and Colin wrestled Braithe up the staircase as he continued to thrash. Arletta and I followed closely behind and together, we hurried away from the chamber. The chamber I'd waited eighteen years to find. Now, I was leaving it without my love.

We stumbled along the network of tunnels and made our way back out into the open, where we headed straight for our ship.

Arletta and I helped Frederick and Colin force Braithe onto the deck and down the staircase to the level beneath. The two brothers forced Braithe inside a cabin and locked the door. Braithe banged against it. Only a few seconds later, his fist smashed through the wood, spraying splinters everywhere.

We looked at each other with wide-eyed panic as he forced the door back open and launched himself toward Arletta—the nearest person to him.

"He's lost his mind," Frederick grunted as he forced Braithe backward, "We're going to have to sedate him somehow… I'm sorry to do this to you, brother." The two brothers worked together in pinning Braithe against the wall. Colin gripped the back of his neck. I looked away as he jerked it backward, snapping his brother's neck.

Braithe fell to the floor, unconscious. The four of us picked him up and carried him back into the room. We laid him on the bed and reentered the corridor, closing the splintered door behind us.

"What now?" I croaked.

"We have maybe twelve to twenty-four hours before Braithe's spine heals," Frederick said. "I'm hoping his behavior was just some kind of reaction to his own brother attacking him." He looked unsettled as he glanced through the hole in the door at the still form of Braithe lying on the bed. "Hopefully, he will have recovered by the time he comes to."

***

After we paralyzed Braithe, the first thing I wanted to do was gather blood and take it to Hans. But Frederick was against it.

"I don't think we should go anywhere near that chamber again until Braithe has recovered," Frederick said as we made our way up to the deck. "In fact, I don't feel comfortable staying near this beach. We'll move further into the ocean and float there for a while."

"Why do we need to wait?" I asked.

"I just..." Frederick hesitated, a look of concern in his eyes. "I have a very bad feeling about this. I just want to see Braithe recovered before we go near that dungeon again."

Colin and Frederick navigated the ship away from Cruor's shore. My eyes stung with tears as I gazed back at the beach.

Once the shoreline had faded into the distance, Frederick guided the sea creatures to a stop while Colin lowered the anchor.

We sat around a table on the upper deck in tense silence. We were all still recovering from the shock of everything we'd just been through.

As the early-morning hours approached, even though we didn't expect Braithe's spine to have recovered yet—in fact, we weren't expecting it to for at least another three hours—Frederick stood up and mumbled that he was going to go check on his brother. The rest of us were too anxious not to accompany him. Leaving our seats and descending to the lower deck together, we froze on the staircase as the corridor came into view. The damaged door behind which Frederick and Colin had laid Braithe on a bed was wide open.

"Didn't we shut that?" Arletta murmured.

"Yes. We left it shut," Frederick answered, daring to move forward again. We reached the bottom of the stairs and peered cautiously through the door into the open room.

It was empty.

My eyes falling to the floor, I noticed clumps of honey brown hair… Braithe's hair?

A snarl came from our right. We twisted to see… *Hans?* A slouching skeletal figure with thin, stark-white skin, and a nose shrunken into its face. He had the same terrifying appearance as my lover and yet he was wearing Braithe's clothes. He was also slightly shorter than Hans.

"Braithe?" Frederick gasped.

His small, dark eyes stared back at us, expressionless. Then he began to shuffle closer toward us, slowly at first, and then picking up speed.

"Run!" Colin yelled, and even though my legs felt numb with shock, I forced myself to race up the stairs. As the five of us bundled out of the trap door leading to the upper deck, we banged it shut behind us.

Frederick swore. "That was Braithe," he said breathlessly. "I don't understand. How—?"

His stumbling words stopped short as the trap door beneath us shuddered. That thing—Braithe—was beginning to attack it. From the force of his blows, I couldn't imagine that it would be more than a minute before he broke through, for it was only made of wood. Frederick and Colin scurried around the deck looking for anything movable and heavy that they could place on top of the door. Apart from the table that they turned upside down and heaved over the door, there really wasn't much else up here that we could use.

"What is going on?" Arletta sobbed.

Wood crunched, and the whole table shifted even as the brothers strained to hold it in place. Sensing what was to come, Frederick yelled toward Arletta and me. "You two, get in the lifeboat and sail away. Hurry!"

"What about you two?" I shot back. "We can't just leave you here!"

"Just get inside and—"

The table went flying upward, sending the two brothers crashing back. Braithe sprang from the trapdoor and scanned the deck. His eyes fell first on Frederick and then Colin. I wasn't sure if he'd noticed Arletta and me, standing all the way on the other side of the deck, but he headed straight for his brothers. He leapt first for Colin and dug his fangs into his neck.

"No!" Arletta and I screamed.

Frederick attempted to haul Braithe off, only to find Braithe attacking him and biting his neck. Both brothers were now groaning with pain, the same deep, guttural groan that Braithe had let out after he'd been attacked by Hans back down near the chamber.

Before I could stop her, Arletta had left my side and shot forward. Grabbing a metal pole along the way, she ran toward Braithe, brandishing the weapon in front of her and waving it, as if she hoped to scare him. "Back off, Braithe!" she screamed. "Don't do this to your brothers!"

She continued holding out the pole directly in front of her, even as Braithe whirled around and fixed his attention on his sister. Staggering forward, he launched right at her. She screamed as the pole pierced Braithe's chest, its tip appearing through his back.

I rushed over and gazed down at Braithe falling to his knees. A thick black substance seeped from his chest, a substance that I could only assume had become his blood.

"I-I killed him!" Arletta stammered, even though she hadn't. Braithe had killed himself. It was like he had lost his mind and run right at her, even though the sharp end of the pole had been extended in front of her.

Braithe's hands moved to the pole in his chest, and his thin fingers closed around it. With a squelch, he yanked, sliding out the pole from his flesh and sending it skidding across the deck.

"He's still alive," Colin panted.

Braithe shot to his feet with alarming speed. *How can this be?* The pole had punctured a hole right through his chest and even through where his heart should have been. *He should be a dead vampire.*

Instead he just sprang up as though nothing had happened. His eyes fixed on Arletta, his almost nonexistent lips curving in a grimace. He lunged toward her. Frederick, even in his pain, managed to leap for Braithe and grab hold of his midriff before he could reach their sister. Frederick wrestled him to the ground, but Braithe caught hold of Frederick's arm and sank his fangs in again. "Both of you, go now!" Frederick yelled. "Escape in the boat!"

As Arletta screamed, I had two choices. I could either join her in screaming or obey Frederick's request to save ourselves. Arletta and I were now only moments away from being attacked. There was no time to lower the boat. Grabbing Arletta's hand, I pulled her to the railing and with one strong push from my legs, I sent us both tumbling over the side of the boat and down into the waves. Still holding onto Arletta's hand, I forced the two of us deep under the water before we swam as fast as we could in the opposite direction from the ship.

I kept looking back over my shoulder every few seconds, opening my eyes even though the saltwater stung, to see if the deathly form of Braithe was following after us. But as we swam further and further away from the ship, my tension eased a little. Finally, after we'd distanced ourselves by at least two miles, I allowed us to resurface to gasp for breath. It was a good thing that vampires could hold their breath for a long time.

We gazed at the distant outline of the ship, listening to the cries of Frederick and Colin. *What is Braithe going to do with them? Will he slaughter them?*

I glanced at Arletta's face, drained of all color. Her lips were parted and trembling. I could see she'd gotten past the stage of screaming, and now her mind was numb with shock.

All I wanted to do was curl up in a ball and sob, but we were now adrift in the ocean. We had to reach land before the sun rose, or Arletta and I would burn. Looking all around us, I decided that we ought to head north. Other than Cruor, where we dared not return, the nearest landmass was in that direction.

I tugged on Arletta. "Come on," I said in a choked whisper. "You need to follow me. We don't have long before the sun rises."

She resisted my urging for several minutes, her eyes remaining fixed on the ship in horror. I slapped her face hard, and that brought her out of her stupor.

"Arletta. I'm a wreck, too. But getting fried in the ocean won't do your brothers any favors."

Mention of her brothers seemed to get through to her. At least she followed me as I continued swimming with all the speed my limbs could muster.

As we swam, the ghastly forms of Hans and Braithe—the same forms that I was now certain Frederick and Colin would soon develop—plagued my mind. My head reeled. What had happened? *What has my Hans become?* It was like the starvation had caused Hans and his fellow vampires to somehow evolve… into a different species altogether. *How is it that Braithe didn't die when the pole struck his heart? No vampire should have survived that. And whatever his condition is, it's contagious?*

It was as though they were no longer even vampires… Or at least, not the vampires we knew.

Chapter 1: Ben

As I finished downing the blue elixir, a fire blazed in my stomach. I dropped the glass bottle. The burning sensation spread from my stomach to my chest, then along my limbs to the tips of my toes and fingers. The Elder's shrieking faded into the background. I closed my eyes tight, locking my jaw as the agony consumed me.

And then, just as I felt that I could take it no longer, it stopped.

A lightness filled me. I felt myself floating upward. I opened my eyes. The sky above me, previously streaked with red, now looked washed out, its vibrant color faded. I twisted, rolling over weightlessly in what felt like midair, to face downward.

Beneath me was... me. My body. Curled up in a fetal position, face and fists clenched up in pain. Perfectly still, surrounded by the shards of the shattered glass vial.

The black mist of the Elder reached my body. He billowed around it, engulfing it completely, even as he continued to screech.

I stared down at my hands. They were a pearly, translucent white, as were my feet... and the rest of my form. I could almost see the dark ground below through my limbs.

When I'd realized my only path lay in taking the potion, I hadn't been completely certain that it would work. That the liquid would really do what Arron had told me it would—detach me from my body and turn me into... a ghost. Although I had prayed that it would, I hadn't been in the slightest bit prepared for it.

I no longer had a body. I was a ghost. A subtle being, trapped in the so-called "in-between" that Arron had described. This was the only place that I could be. I couldn't remain in my body without putting into jeopardy not just the human realm, but countless others. And at the same time, I wasn't ready to meet with death...

Staring down at my body curled up on the ground shook me to the core.

I am down there... and yet I am not.

Then what am I?

Throughout my existence, since the day I was born, I'd identified myself with that body, the body I now saw lying on the ground, a corpse. Although the Hawk had told me that I had an existence separate from it, being told such a thing and actually experiencing it were two different matters entirely. *Arron was right. Although devoid of my physical wrapping, I still possess thoughts. Mind. Consciousness. There is more to each of us than flesh and bone.*

The Elder, still swirling around my body, was apparently trying to enter it. But he remained outside—it was no longer habitable to him. They couldn't inhabit corpses. They could only hijack bodies that were still living.

The Elder tried in vain for several moments before, letting out another scream of frustration, he moved away from my body. Apparently having accepted that there was no way I could be of use to him anymore, he began to glide away toward the edge of the cliff... when another presence arrived—another veil of black mist, followed by a voice.

"What happened to the boy?" the hiss asked Basilius.

"This is all a result of the girl vessel's incompetence." Basilius' voice dripped with rage. "She allowed him to carry an elixir all this time. He took it moments before I was able to enter him, and now... Now he is lost to us! All those years we waited, gone to waste! His corpse lies there, frozen and useless. Julie Duan is not to be shown her lover. She must be punished for this grievous error."

"It is too late for that. I have already taken her to him," the second voice replied.

Basilius screeched again.

"However," the second Elder continued, "I assure you that her visit to the mountain chamber just now was indeed a punishment."

"What?"

"I had taken Julie Duan to see her lover, as you promised her, and she was met with anything but relief… We discovered something… peculiar and wondrous."

"What did you discover?" Basilius asked, his voice anxious.

"I wish to show you rather than describe it. Let us go now."

The two dark presences lingered a little longer, as Basilius roamed over my body once more, before both of them vanished.

I didn't understand half of their conversation, though the Elder's words regarding Julie reuniting with her lover registered in my brain. Still, I couldn't pay much attention to it. My mind already felt close to explosion, if it had not blown already.

I reached out my hands, then tried to shift my legs, in an attempt to discover how much control I had over my movements. I willed myself to drift downwards, moving my legs as though I were walking, and effortlessly, I descended to my body.

I extended a hand down to touch my shoulder. My fingers sank right through it. I tried to push against my side, roll my body so that I lay on my back. Again, it was like trying to push air.

My mind was in a state of shock as I tried to process this new state of being. I drifted upward again, regaining a bird's eye view of my body.

What do I do now?

I cast my eyes over my pale surroundings in desperation.

Although I understood that I had separated from my body and now had a new existence outside of it, I still felt somehow… tied to it. Bound by some kind of invisible rope.

How can I just leave my body here? What will happen to it?

Will it rot like a regular human corpse? Will it become nothing but dust, leaving me trapped in this subtle existence forever?

I felt frozen, my mind in a state of paralysis.

I couldn't have known how much time I spent hovering over my body. Time had lost its meaning. It could have been hours, days, or possibly even weeks that I haunted that spot, held hostage by a chain I was too terrified to sever.

This body beneath me was the last link I had with my former life. With any life. It felt like I was hanging onto the edge of a gaping black hole—this body being the last grip I had before slipping into an endless oblivion.

I hovered, feeling no sensation. No coldness. No heat. No pain. I just felt numb. All the while, my body remained stiff and still, showing no signs yet of deterioration.

Eventually, I came to terms with the idea that I couldn't stay here forever. I had to leave, even though it felt like leaving half of me behind. I couldn't stay haunting this ghastly realm for all eternity, as though I was an Elder myself. I had to break away, even though I had no idea what that would mean for me, what was to become of my life—if what I was experiencing could even be considered a life.

Summoning up every ounce of willpower that I possessed, I drifted away from my corpse. My form floated away from the clifftop and over the steep drop. Even as I moved toward the shore, my eyes remained fixed on my body until it was nothing but a speck in the distance.

As I sensed the ocean miles beneath me, it took all the strength I had to turn my back on the mountains and face the wide-open water.

I tried to calm my mind and focus my consciousness on the only question that mattered anymore:

What now?

Chapter 2: Sofia

I was surprised to discover that Cyrus was the leader of the Drizan jinn. I hadn't expected that a person of such importance would come to meet us outside personally, rather than some lower member of the family.

Jeriad apparently shared my surprise, and he voiced it to the formidable-looking jinni. Cyrus replied with a gracious smile that he had sensed the presence of dragons, and that it was right that he should come to greet them personally—since, after all, they did have a history together.

Although I didn't trust anything about this jinni, at least we could be sure about one thing—he and his clan clearly still held respect for the dragons and didn't see them as a threat.

And consequently the rest of us were also welcomed in. Derek and I—along with Rose, Caleb, Aiden, the Novalics, Ashley, Landis, Zinnia, Gavin, and other close companions who'd traveled with us—found ourselves descending the jeweled staircase, which led down into a grand entrance hall. The luxury that surrounded us was similar to that of the Nasiri jinn's abode at the bottom of The Oasis—no expense had been spared, and if it was possible, this place held even more extravagance, at least what we'd seen of it so far. The hall's floor appeared to be made of solid gold, covered every now and then by rugs so soft they felt like pure cashmere. Gem-studded mirrors adorned the walls and diamond-encrusted chandeliers hung from the ceiling in abundance.

We moved out of this room and entered a corridor, similarly decorated. It was wide, with grand pillars lining the walls every few feet. There was a scent of burning incense, subtle yet heady.

Although it shared its luxury with the Nasiris' abode, the Drizans' was not an atrium. It was more like a palace, built underground.

Finally, the jinn stopped outside a tall, open doorway. We entered to find ourselves in some kind of old-fashioned courtroom, lit by beacons of fire. Opposite us was a raised platform upon which sat a silver throne embroidered with crimson silk. Above this throne, hanging from the wall, was another large golden medallion with the symbol of a scorpion—like the one that served as the entrance to the Drizans' lair. Its shiny surface glimmered in the firelight. Cyrus glided up to the throne and planted himself down on it, eyeing us all from his vantage point.

"Take seats if you like," he said, his deep voice booming around the chamber. As soon as he uttered the words, dozens of chairs manifested and lined up on the floor beneath his platform. The dragons—having already shifted back into their humanoid forms in order to fit through the entrance—remained standing, as did the rest of us. It appeared that our nerves didn't permit any of us to sit.

"We will stand, but thank you for the offer," Jeriad replied.

"As you wish," Cyrus said. "So, what exactly have you come to tell me?" Cyrus folded his fingers around the arms of his chair. "Our fellow jinn, the Nasiris. You say that they have settled in the human realm?"

"Indeed," Jeriad replied coolly. "The Nasiri jinn have formed a bond with a friend of mine. He is a vampire, and they have managed to bond him to them permanently. We seek your help in freeing him and in return, I will inform you of their location and anything else we know about them that could be of use to you."

The jinni's eyes glinted with interest as he raised a hand to his chin and stroked it. "I guessed that Nuriya had fled to the human realm… In fact, some years ago I even sent out a search party looking for her. But they returned unsuccessful. I always wondered where she'd managed to hide out so successfully all this time…" He stood up, his hand still against his chin, and began pacing thoughtfully along his platform.

"You see, Nuriya and I… we have something of a history together," Cyrus continued. "Once upon a time, she was my betrothed. Her father, the noble Harith Nasiri, had gifted her to me as a gesture of goodwill between our two dynasties. However, Nuriya was a treacherous woman. She slighted not only her father's will but also mine, and fell into the arms of another man. A lowly slave, at that. The disgrace she brought upon her father caused him to disown her, and of course the offense caused to myself and my own lineage meant that I was bound to mete out my own punishment on her… For you see, these are the ways of the jinn."

He paused, biting his lower lip, his eyes coming alive at the memory. "After her father expelled her, she fled with the slave—Freiyus was his name—and a small entourage whose loyalty lay with the young whore, rather than with her esteemed family. They formed a home together, still within the country of the jinn yet some distance away, thinking that they could hide from us. Of course, we hunted them down and found them in the end… We did what we had to do with those who resided with the women, but Nuriya herself, being the slithering snake that she is, slid out of my grasp once again. She escaped the raid and left The Dunes entirely. I suspected she might have fled to the human realm, though we never did know for sure."

He looked back toward Jeriad, another smile curving his full lips. "So you see, dragon, your visit is quite welcome. And once you disclose the Nasiris' location, I will be quite happy to assist you in freeing this friend of yours from the jinn's bond. In fact, after I am finished with Nuriya and whoever else she's holed up with, I doubt any of them will have the strength to bond again..."

"I'm glad to hear it," Jeriad replied, clearing his throat. He turned to glance at Derek and me briefly before his focus resumed on the jinni. "When would we be able to leave? I am anxious to reclaim this friend of mine."

"I, too, am anxious to leave—that much I assure you," Cyrus replied. "I suggest that we leave within an hour. It won't take long to gather up my army. In the meantime, please wait here and make yourselves comfortable." A table appeared in front of us, lined with dozens of crystal glasses and silver jugs. "Help yourselves to refreshments, and I will return to inform you when we are ready to leave."

With that, he vanished.

I released a breath I hadn't realized I'd been holding. I

turned to my husband and slowly raised a brow. "What do you think?"

Derek's forehead was furrowed. "I don't know what to make of this jinni. I don't trust him in the slightest—just as I don't trust any of his kind. But Jeriad seems to trust him. Only time will tell whether Cyrus can help us free Benjamin from the Nasiris' bond."

I nodded, gulping. "I guess I'm just trying to think of what could go wrong… I suppose not much, right? I mean, I can't see how the situation could get any worse than Ben being bound eternally to those jinn. I can only imagine that good can come of this…" Even as I said the words, doubt gripped me.

"I can only assume so," Derek replied, a similar unsettled expression on his face.

After that, all of us passed the next hour waiting in mostly silence for Cyrus to return. Some of the vampires—Rose and Ashley at the lead—considered the jinni's offer of refreshments. But the jugs were filled with human blood. I could hardly remember the last time I'd relished the sweet delicacy, but as much as the blood called to me, there was no way I could give into the urge. I simply couldn't. I was pleased to see that my daughter, Ashley and everyone else also refrained once they realized that it was human blood. Just two decades ago, the older vampires in this room wouldn't have thought twice about chugging down the human blood. Now, after practicing abstinence from it for so long and training their murderous nature, they were averse to it even when it was presented to them—quite literally—on a silver platter.

When Cyrus returned, he manifested himself in the same spot he had left, just in front of his throne.

"We are ready," he said, a hint of excitement in his voice. "Let us return to the sand above, where my army is waiting."

He led us out of the door, retracing the same path he'd taken in bringing us down here. Climbing up the jeweled staircase, we emerged back in the desert of black sand. Surrounding us was a huge swarm of jinn. It took my breath away to see how many there were. They each shared similar features: smooth ebony skin and heavily set jaws—heavier than the Nasiris'. The women had tightly curled hair, and most of the men were bald—some sporting immaculately sculpted goatees.

"So tell me, Jeriad." Cyrus faced the shifter. "How exactly do you propose to lead us to the Nasiris?"

"We dragons must fly by our own strength, of course," Jeriad replied. *Of course, I forgot.* "For as you know, we do not accept transport from magical beings. You may fly with us on our backs, for there is plenty of space. Or, if you wish to fly using your own powers, you can soar alongside us."

"We shall soar alongside you," Cyrus replied after a

moment of thought.

"Our destination in the human realm is a country called Egypt," Jeriad said. "The Nasiris reside in a desert, whose name is… I forget these human names." Jeriad looked toward Derek.

"The Sahara Desert," Derek prompted.

"Then pray, lead us there," Cyrus said. "Since we're not traveling by magic, it will take some time, and I am most eager to reunite with old acquaintances…"

***

We returned through the same portal that we had arrived through, on the beach in the country of ogres. Traveling with supernatural speed—the jinn soaring at the dragons' side—it wasn't long before we arrived back in the Sahara Desert. The spell of shade that was cast upon us before we left The Shade was still active, though my throat still felt parched as we descended and touched down on the sand. The jinn cast their eyes about, scanning the area expectantly. We walked around the dunes until we located The Oasis' boundary.

"Interesting," Cyrus said, laying his hands flat against the invisible wall. "This is where she has been all this time… Do you know how many jinn live here?"

Jeriad looked to Derek and me for an answer. I shrugged. We really hadn't spent much time down there. It was hard to give even an estimate. From the look on Derek's face, he wasn't sure either.

"We aren't certain," I replied. "But if I had to take a wild guess, I would say at least a dozen."

"A dozen," Cyrus said thoughtfully, more to himself than to anyone else. "I wonder if more outcasts joined her..."

He ran his hands along the barrier before he cleared his throat and addressed his jinn companions in a low voice. "We're strong enough to break through this together." He turned to Jeriad. "I suggest that the rest of you stand back. Far back."

Derek's hand slid into mine as we all moved backward with the dragons, while the jinn moved forward and lined up against the barrier. They adopted the same stance as Cyrus—shoulders squared, palms resting against the invisible wall.

A moment later, there was a searing flash of light, so bright that I feared for Derek's human eyes. I reached instinctively for his neck and tugged him to face the opposite direction.

Once the light had faded, Derek and I, along with Rose, Caleb, Aiden and the other vampires, faced The Oasis. The boundary had been broken and now we could see what had been hidden beyond its walls. My eyes fixed on the camel stable before roaming the ground in search of the trap door. We soon spotted it. Approaching it, we discovered that it was locked.

The jinn emitted another painful flash of light and the trap door popped open obediently.

The sound of scurrying came from beneath us, footsteps echoing across marble floors, in the vampires' atrium. I could only assume they had already detected our intrusion. Cyrus was about to descend toward the lower levels when Derek spoke up.

"Wait," he said. "A coven of vampires live in this upper atrium and it's not necessary to cause harm to them. The jinn are the ones who hold the boy in question—my son—as a prisoner. These vampires are mere puppets. I would also request that you leave all humans alone."

I understood the motive behind Derek's words. Of course, he wasn't the harsh ruler he'd been when I met him, and he didn't want to cause unnecessary bloodshed. But he also knew that Lucas' son, Jeramiah, lived here. Derek regretted the hateful relationship he'd had with his brother, and he didn't want to make an enemy out of Jeramiah, who, at least so far, didn't appear to have played much of a role in Ben's troubles. If anything, Jeramiah himself was under the control of the jinn.

"We have no interest in the vampires," Cyrus said. "Nor much in the humans… Just tell us where to find the Nasiris."

"Beneath this atrium lies a prison filled with humans," Derek replied. "Beneath that is where the Nasiris reside."

The jinn glided down the stairs that led from the desert to

the top level of the atrium, whose walls were made of glass, giving us a view of the many levels below. Dark figures streaked across the verandas—vampires, carrying weapons, and all moving in our direction.

One of them looked upward—a young woman with thick blonde hair—and the moment she laid eyes on the jinn a scream escaped her lips.

"Enemy jinn!" She began yelling to her companions and pointing up toward the jinn standing and watching behind the glass. "Retreat!"

More vampires stopped in their tracks and gazed up at us, their faces filling with fear and dread. They scattered in all directions as they hurried toward doors and locked themselves inside apartments. All of these vampires were clearly well accustomed to the might of the jinn.

Even as the jinn flattened the doors leading down to the prison, neither Derek and I nor any of our other companions knew exactly how to reach the Nasiris' home. Although we had been here before, we had been transported by the jinn's magic—not by foot—so we'd never come to know of its exact location. Ben, however, had described the entrance to us briefly—deep in the network of cells, in a small storage room, hidden behind a cabinet. We described these details to Cyrus, and strangely, now that we were down here it was almost as though he didn't need them. He began leading us all forward with a surprisingly strong sense of direction. As we moved, I couldn't help but notice with a shudder the looks of hunger on the jinn's faces as they eyed the humans we passed by.

The jinn's speed picked up and the rest of us had to run to follow. After what felt like half an hour, Cyrus drew us all to a halt outside a narrow door. He pushed it open to reveal a small storage room. The jinni raised a hand for silence and sniffed the air.

Then he nodded. "This is the room your son spoke of. I can feel their closeness."

There wasn't enough room for all of us to step inside at once, so Cyrus and three other jinn moved in first. They shoved the cupboard to one side. Sure enough, behind it was the secret door Ben had spoken of. Cyrus forced it open.

We found ourselves at the top of a small staircase and, descending in single file, we made our way down to a beautiful kitchen. The aroma of exotic spices still lingered in the air from the family's last meal.

We crossed to the other side of the kitchen and emerged in the magnificent atrium. Cyrus's face was impassive as he took in the heavenly abode.

My grip around Derek's hand tightened, the thought of reuniting with my son filling me with anticipation.

Cyrus looked around at his companions and nodded. They nodded back, and although no words were exchanged, they appeared to know what to do. They rushed forward at once, sweeping toward the nearest line of doors like a wave.

There were screams. Shouts. The crash of furniture and bang of doors. More jinn flooded into rooms. There were so many of the Drizan jinn present, soon every level was swarming with them. My daughter, father and the other vampires moved with the dragons to stand safely in the central gardens on our request, while Derek and I followed Cyrus in search of Queen Nuriya herself.

Cyrus' instinct was that her apartment would be right at the top, and it appeared that he was right. We stopped in front of a door that was larger and more heavily ornamented than all the others. The jinni lost no time in breaking down the door.

Before entering, he whirled back round to face us. "Wait here," he said. "I will handle this alone."

And so Derek and I hung back. I peered anxiously down the shadowy corridor of Nuriya's apartment as Cyrus disappeared down it. A few seconds later came a bloodcurdling scream.

"No!"

The anguish in the queen's cry chilled me to the bone.

"Please, Cyrus! Don't do this to me! Not again!"

As much as I resented the jinni for what she'd done to my son, and needed the bond to be broken, her cries of fear and pleas were hard to swallow. I didn't want to think about what he was doing to her as her screams intensified.

"You've already taken so much from me," she sobbed. "Don't take my family. Please! Don't wreck me again! I've suffered enough."

Cyrus hissed, "Not enough."

"Freiyus is dead! You killed him along with our newborn! Take me, but spare my family this time. Please! They have done nothing to harm you!"

Her pleas clawed at my chest and I found myself slightly out of breath. "What is he doing to her?" I murmured, a sick feeling settling into the pit of my stomach.

Derek gave me a dark look.

As Nuriya's voice broke from her pleading, I couldn't handle it anymore. I left Derek's side and ran into the apartment.

"Sofia!" Derek hissed, hurrying after me.

I sprinted down the corridor to a bedroom whose door was left open. Nuriya, draped in a midnight-blue nightgown, now torn and awry, was being pinned up against the wall by Cyrus. His hands were clamped around her neck. Part of me wondered why she didn't vanish, but I guessed Cyrus' powers ensured that she couldn't.

I stood rooted to the spot, staring at the couple. Before I could have second thoughts about my intrusion, Nuriya spotted me over Cyrus' shoulder.

"You're Ben's birth mother," she gasped.

Cyrus twisted around to face us, a look of irritation in his eyes.

"Why are you here?" he asked. "I told you to wait outside."

"Come on, Sofia," Derek said, having arrived behind me.

Even as my husband gripped my arm and tugged at me, I couldn't take my eyes off of Nuriya's terrified face.

"Where is my son?" I asked her.

She appeared to have reached levels of hysteria too high for her answer to be coherent. "Please!" she called to me. "Don't let him do this to me! I only want the best for Benjamin. I only ever wanted to protect him, to make him my own! I've nurtured and helped him like he was born of my own womb, in ways that you never could. P-Please, don't let the Drizans destroy my family!"

It shook me how she was crying to me as though I was the one who had her by the neck. Of course, Derek and I were responsible for this raid. We were the ones who'd instigated it.

Cyrus' hand closed hard around the jinni's neck, strangling her voice.

"Did you not hear me, vampire?" he asked, his dark eyes digging into mine. "I asked you to leave. Fear not about your son. I will find your son, wherever he is in this place, and bring him to you. The Nasiris will be weakened, and their bond with him will be broken. Now go wait with the others in the gardens."

Beneath the surface of his politeness bubbled intense irritation. After all, in his eyes, it was none of my business what transpired between the two. His end of the deal was simply to free our son, no matter what method he chose to use.

"Come on, Sofia," Derek said through gritted teeth. He placed an arm around my waist and led me out of the room, even as I felt torn.

From the little that I'd gleaned about Nuriya's life before she'd taken refuge in The Oasis, it had been a miserable existence. She'd been forced to marry someone she didn't love while her heart belonged to another man who wasn't socially acceptable. Then she'd been kicked out by her father, and then hounded by this Cyrus beast… who'd killed not only her lover but also her newborn child.

My son had told me about her obsession with family and holding people close to her, as though they were her own flesh and blood. She was obviously traumatized by the events of her past. And although she was keeping Benjamin trapped in her world, my heart went out to her. I knew what it felt like to lose a newborn. I'd gone through the torture of losing two. It was a feeling I wouldn't wish upon my worst enemy.

Even though I let Derek lead me back outside the apartment, my mind remained in the bedroom as Cyrus continued to taunt and torture the desperate woman. I turned my back on the front door, clutching the railing.

Derek stood by my side and placed his hand over mine on the railing.

"Sofia," he said, gripping my shoulders and twisting me to face him. His blue eyes looked down seriously into mine. "This woman is keeping our son as a prisoner here. Don't forget that."

With that, he caught my hand and walked back down the levels to join Aiden, Rose, Caleb and the other vampires, who were waiting with the dragons in the center of the gardens, while the Drizan jinn finished raiding the atrium. They'd lined up dozens of Nasiri jinn against the walls, bound by their wrists in some kind of glowing, bright green rope. I hated to think about what the Drizans' plan might be for them now. *Will they murder them?*

I should have been relieved that we were closer than ever to getting Ben back, but my stomach was twisted up in knots. Yes, Derek was right that she'd imprisoned our son, but this lady clearly had issues. And she hadn't done anything to actually harm Benjamin. If anything, she had protected him on his journey from Egypt to The Shade. She wanted to look after him, adopt him as her own son. As unnerving as these powerful creatures were, at least with Nuriya, I didn't get the sense that she was malicious. She seemed to be just… broken.

And as a woman, a mother, I could relate to her in a way that Derek couldn't. She was clearly still suffering from trauma and for us to storm in here like this and be the cause of Cyrus abusing her… I swallowed hard, recalling the way she'd looked at me back in the bedroom. She'd seemed so weak, so helpless, as she was being tortured physically and psychologically by a man twice her size… And Derek and I had just left. No matter what grudge I held against her, this just didn't seem humane on our part.

"There has to be another way of doing this," I said, looking around at the rows of bound Nasiri jinn. Each of them looked petrified, with some of the younger jinn crying for their mothers. In spite of what they'd done, these jinn in The Oasis were just another family.

"What other way?" Derek asked. "Besides, it's too late to backtrack now."

He was right. As much as I hated what we were doing to these creatures, I couldn't think of any other way but force. Nuriya was so attached to Ben that she'd formed this strong bond that would tie him to her for his entire life. Ben himself had been convinced that there was no negotiating to be done, that it was set in stone.

I rested my head against Derek's chest, trying to shut out

the horrible scene around me. When Jeriad had made the offer of help to Derek, I hadn't thought that it would be such a violent route as this. I'd thought that perhaps Jeriad's jinn acquaintances might be able to help us in some other way, perhaps via a friendly connection of Nuriya's who might put in a good word for us and persuade her to let Ben go. I had been so anxious to accept Jeriad's proposal, since there was nothing else on the table, that I hadn't stopped to consider what exactly this would involve.

"Let's just hope we're reunited with Ben soon," Rose murmured to my right. She held my hand and squeezed it.

Ten minutes later, it appeared that the Drizans had emptied every single chamber. They piled out of the apartments and gathered around the Nasiris being held captive on the ground. Some of the younger Drizan jinn dipped down to poke and taunt the Nasiri cruelly. I had half a mind to snap at them to stop, but I knew that wouldn't help.

"Now we're just waiting for Cyrus," Derek muttered.

"They're coming." Aiden pointed toward the staircase nearest to us.

The towering form of Cyrus descended the stairs, carrying Nuriya in his arms. He'd tied her with the same strange rope the other jinn had been bound by. Her cries of anguish on seeing her family lined up along the wall were muffled by a gag in her mouth. She coughed and choked.

Cyrus laid Nuriya down on the ground in front of the rest of the Nasiri jinn, and, to my surprise, removed her gag. Perhaps he enjoyed the sound of her sobbing.

I tried to avoid looking at the queen, seeing as there was nothing I could think of to alleviate her suffering or prevent the Drizans' path of vengeance. To my dismay, she addressed me directly, forcing me to look up.

"Benjamin's birth mother," she gasped, as though she didn't know my name. "You don't understand. My darling Ben is in grave danger. He needs us. If you let the Drizans have their way with us, your son will be lost to you forever. Bahir is with him now protecting him, but he will sense my pain and leave Ben. If that happens, oh! I can't bear to think of it! He'll be left stranded and—"

"Enough!" Cyrus snapped. He stuffed the gag back in her mouth.

The blood drained from my face. "What?" I choked, staring down at Nuriya. "What do you mean, Ben's in danger? Where is he? What happened to him?"

I stumbled forward, ignoring the angered expression on Cyrus's face as I reached down to pull the gag from Nuriya's mouth. But, bizarrely, as much as I tugged, it was stuck fast. I turned to Cyrus with pleading eyes.

"I need to hear what this jinni has to say about my son," I

breathed. "Please, remove the gag."

Cyrus' eyes smoldered as he looked from me to Nuriya. Then he turned on Jeriad, whose face remained stoic as he witnessed the scene. Cyrus' jaw twitched as he stooped down and pulled out the gag.

Nuriya coughed and spluttered, tears streaming down her cheeks.

I bent down to her level and touched her shoulder. It felt surprisingly solid for such an ethereal creature, and I gripped it hard.

"Where is Benjamin? He'll be left stranded where? Are you saying that he's not here in The Oasis?"

Nuriya bit down on her trembling lip and nodded. "He's not here. After you left, an oracle informed us of something terrible about Benjamin." She swallowed hard. "The Elders intend to make him their slave for eternity. They want him for themselves—they have since he was a newborn. An Elder imprinted on him when he was an infant and formed a bond that would connect the two of them for as long as Benjamin's heart remained beating. Ben is currently in the supernatural dimension with Aisha, my niece, and Bahir, my partner, trying to find a way to get rid of the bond that the Elder formed with him. The Elder is calling Benjamin back to Cruor, and since he drank so much human blood recently, the spirit has become strong enough to take control of Ben's body like never before. I don't know exactly where they are now in the supernatural world, but Bahir is inside Ben, battling the Elder to keep his mind from being taken over. If I continue to be harassed, Bahir will sense my disturbance and come for me. He might be on his way already! Benjamin *needs* two jinn with him!"

Her words left me speechless. I froze, kneeling on the floor and gaping at the jinni.

My son, bonded to an Elder?

"What does the Elder want with him?" Derek asked, shock shaking his voice.

"He wants to use Ben to nurse himself back to health and help all the Elders rise up. Other vessels are of no use to them, for they are too weak to inhabit regular vessels. But Ben's Elder, Basilius, managed to form a special bond which allowed him to gain nourishment from the blood Ben consumed. If he manages to lure Ben back to Cruor, he will certainly be strong enough to inhabit Benjamin and take him over fully."

"When did he leave?" I asked, shaking her shoulders. "How long has he been gone?"

"Days now," she replied.

Oh, no. No. Not my son.

I'd often feared that something bad had happened to Ben while he'd been in Aviary, but nothing could have prepared me for this.

Nuriya had every reason to lie to us regarding Ben in order to save her and her family's skin from the Drizan jinn. But something in her eyes made me believe that she was telling the truth. As hard as it was to swallow, Ben having been bonded to an Elder would explain a lot of things, like why he was the only vampire we'd ever come across who couldn't physically stomach animal blood.

And if there was even the smallest chance that Nuriya was speaking the truth, breaking Benjamin's bond with the jinn would actually do more harm than good. Possibly irreparable harm. I clenched my jaw at the irony. This bond created by jinn that had caused me so much pain before now appeared to be his saving grace. And by trying to cut it off, we were cutting off my son.

The Drizans had to stop with their raid.

I faced the agitated Cyrus. Even though I knew this monster would never agree to it, I couldn't help but try. "Your lordship, we must call this off. Your actions could be greatly injuring my son, for if Nuriya speaks the truth, he is bonded to a much worse force than the jinn."

The tension that had been building between Cyrus and me since I'd entered Nuriya's bedroom while he tortured her reached breaking point. He whirled around to glare at Jeriad.

"What is this, dragon?" he seethed, fire in his eyes. "I

cannot tolerate this vampire any longer. None of this was part of our deal. We agreed to extricate the young man from the Nasiris' clutches, and that was all. What we choose to do with these traitors is none of your business."

I looked pleadingly at Jeriad, but what could the dragon shifter do? We had already entered into an agreement with the Drizans on the strength of the goodwill the dragons had built with the jinn over the years. Their willingness to bend to the dragons' requests only stretched so far.

"Please," I croaked, not sure what other option I had left but to beg for any scrap of compassion this hard-hearted jinni might possess. "Just... stop harassing the Nasiris. At least for now."

Cyrus shrugged me off. He moved closer to Nuriya and replaced the gag in her mouth even as she sobbed. Then he turned his back on us completely and looked around at his jinn companions. "We return now to the palace. Make sure that not a single Nasiri gets left behind."

He scooped up Nuriya again in his arms and, shooting one last glare my way, vanished. He was followed a moment later by the rest of the Drizan jinn, carrying the Nasiri captives in their arms, leaving me, Derek and our small army standing alone in the magnificent atrium.

Jeriad approached Derek and me, his piercing, aquamarine-blue eyes meeting mine. "Queen Sofia. Backing out of an agreement with jinn is simply not done."

"So where is his end of the agreement?" Rose asked. "He's supposed to find Ben for us."

Jeriad glanced at my daughter. "I suspect that he sensed the truth in Nuriya's words, that Benjamin is no longer in The Oasis. His agreement was to break the bond and return Ben to us, on the understanding that Ben would actually be here. He never said he'd go hunting elsewhere for your brother...."

I stared at my husband, and I could see from his blood-drained face that the same question was running through both our minds. *What now?*

Benjamin was trapped somewhere in the supernatural dimension, and if what Nuriya said came to pass, Bahir would leave him, and he wouldn't have enough protection to stop the Elder from calling him to Cruor... *What will become of my son?*

Chapter 3: Derek

I wanted to resist taking Nuriya's words seriously. I wanted to believe she'd spoken them solely out of desperation, in an attempt to save her and her family, and Benjamin was still here somewhere in The Oasis. Yet another part of me sensed the truth in the jinni's words, even despite her desperate situation. What she'd told us about Ben just… made sense. I recalled the vision that Ben had shortly before we'd all left The Shade for The Oasis. He'd described Cruor in vivid detail, and of a dark presence engulfing him as a newborn. The pieces of Benjamin's mystery fell into place in my mind.

And yet I wasn't ready to resign myself to Ben's fate.

"We need to do a thorough search of this place," I spoke

up, glancing around at our companions. "Search every nook and cranny."

We split up and began making our way around the massive atrium, searching through sprawling apartment after apartment. We checked every room, in cupboards, under beds, but Ben was nowhere to be found down here.

"Perhaps he's being kept in the upper atrium," Aiden muttered.

"Let's search there now," Sofia replied anxiously.

We hurried back into the kitchen and climbed up the narrow staircase toward the prison above.

"Maybe he's in one of these cells," Sofia whispered, gazing around the dimly lit prison corridors. This network of cells was like a labyrinth. There were so many small chambers that it took us a long time to complete the task, even with all of us splitting up in search parties and moving with supernatural speed. Ashley straying from Landis and getting lost didn't help.

Once we were certain that Benjamin was not down here in the cells, our last hope remained with the upper atrium. My throat tightened as we climbed the final staircase leading up to the prison's exit. *The atrium above is where Jeramiah lives.* I still hadn't gotten used to the idea of Lucas having a son, much less the idea of meeting my nephew in person. I wondered how much Jeramiah would look like my brother, and whether he would sound like him.

I swallowed as we entered the upper atrium's gardens. This place looked different now compared to when the Maslens had inhabited it all those years ago. It was a bizarre feeling to be standing here, in the same place where that fateful night occurred. The night I'd rescued Sofia from the hands of Borys Maslen, the night that Benjamin Hudson and my brother had lost their lives.

"I suggest we enter the gardens to keep ourselves positioned centrally while we scope this place out," Aiden spoke up.

We took his suggestion and entered a rose garden nearby, eyeing the various levels of the atrium. We'd been to this upper atrium only recently, but we had been trapped by the powers of the jinn, and we hadn't had a chance to walk around and explore the place. Before we launched into another search for Ben, we needed to get a better feeling for the scope of the atrium. Because looking for him here wouldn't be as simple—it was packed with vampires. Though there were no bloodsuckers to be seen walking around. I guessed that spotting the Drizan jinn had given them such a scare that they were still locked in their apartments, not daring to come out.

We wound our way through an orchard and several ornamental gardens before we arrived at a large pond. Rose stopped near the edge of it and stared down at a slab of stone set among the green grass. I walked toward her to see what it was. A memorial stone. *Lucas Dominic Novak*. Benjamin had mentioned this memorial stone during his recounting of his stay here in The Oasis. Jeramiah must have installed the slab in honor of his father.

We finished passing through the gardens, arriving at the other end of the atrium. Still, none of us detected a single vampire out on the verandas.

I feared that disturbing them in their homes would quickly descend into a fight. They were spooked after seeing us accompanied by the Drizans, but if we started barging into their apartments, they would get defensive. We had to handle the situation delicately, in spite of how desperate Sofia and I were.

"We should just go around knocking on their doors," Sofia said, eyeing the nearest apartment to us. "We'll address them calmly and explain that we're not here to cause any trouble—we're merely looking for Ben."

"Or Joseph, which was what Ben called himself during his stay with these vampires," Rose added. I wasn't sure if the vampires were still ignorant of Benjamin's real identity or if the jinn had finally informed them.

The vampires and I split up again into small groups, while the dragon shifters remained in the gardens. I didn't think that bringing those menacing men to the vampires' doorsteps would help.

We began knocking on doors, and surprisingly, our method worked. They were alarmed to see us, and asked many questions, but nobody tried to fight us. Nobody knew where Joseph, or Benjamin, was either. We insisted on searching inside their apartments, which they allowed us to do, albeit begrudgingly, as long as we were quick about it. They also warned us that if we dared touch a single one of their humans, they'd wage war on us. We were accompanied by dragon shifters, and we would have won in a struggle, but I reminded myself of how The Shade used to be, before Sofia came along. If we freed the humans from the cells, these vampires would only find new innocent victims tomorrow. Surviving on human blood was how they chose to live, and as much as we had all changed in The Shade, attempting to force our rules on them wouldn't change a thing. As Sofia and I discussed the matter, I could see that the suggestion of simply wiping out these Oasis vampires was near the tip of her tongue, but she didn't say it. She never was one to encourage violence as a solution, and she knew what slaughtering my brother's son and his entire coven would do to me.

Reluctantly, we left the matter behind and continued moving from chamber to chamber. We even came across a handful of witches, though they didn't attempt to harm us with their magic. We avoided answering as many questions as possible and moved about the rooms in silence.

In the end, I didn't find myself face to face with Jeramiah.

But we didn't find Ben either.

After one last sweep around the layered verandas, we admitted defeat and headed back to the desert.

"What about the camel stable up in the desert?" Rose suggested desperately.

Although none of us really expected him to be there, we searched the camel stable. Ben wasn't there.

Sofia and I locked eyes. There was no point in fooling ourselves any longer. We weren't going to find Benjamin in The Oasis.

"I believe that Nuriya was speaking truth." Jeriad spoke up, breaking through the tense silence. "We dragons can detect liars by a mere glance into their eyes. And I didn't detect untruth in Nuriya's gaze. I believe that your son indeed left here and is in the supernatural dimension."

But we had no idea where. Or what state he would be in now, if Bahir had left him as Nuriya had feared.

I clutched a palm to my forehead, closing my eyes and trying to focus my mind.

I let out a breath.

"All right," I said heavily. "With Jeriad's assurance, we're going to assume that what Nuriya told Sofia is correct. We've been wasting our time… I have not the first clue in hell what we can do now, if anything, to help my son. But before we do anything, we ought to return to The Shade."

Chapter 4: Derek

As we traveled back to our island, the dragons' supernatural speed didn't seem fast enough. As I'd admitted to everyone, I didn't have any semblance of a plan for how to help my son. And the thought that we had just made things worse for him by getting the Nasiris kidnapped by the Drizans was eating away at me. What would happen to him without the protection of two jinn? Would the Elder really manage to draw him back to Cruor? The latter shouldn't even have been a question, for I knew the kind of powers the Elders could have over a person—I knew them too well. I was just fumbling for some hope in this predicament.

When we finally reached The Shade, I was glad that it was

overcast again. The spell that Ibrahim had cast over us to keep us in shadow while we were gone had lasted till now, but I didn't want any hunters detecting our movements.

The dragons remained above the clouds until we were past the boundary, then descended upon The Shade, silently and gracefully. They touched down in the clearing before the Port.

We had been gone longer than I'd hoped, and the first thing I wanted to do was check on my sister and Xavier. I wondered if Vivienne might have given birth already. But aside from checking that she was in good health, and possibly meeting my new niece or nephew, I needed to see how they'd been holding up since we'd been gone.

Sofia and I hurried through the forest to the couple's penthouse. The lights were on, but as we knocked, nobody answered. Sofia couldn't detect even the slightest sound of anyone inside. The door hadn't been locked. I pushed it open and we stepped inside. We moved from room to room, seeing if they might have left a note for us as to their whereabouts in case we returned.

"Derek," Sofia called from Vivienne and Xavier's bedroom. I hurried to the room to find her pointing to a wet patch on the bed. "I'm guessing Viv's water broke already. Maybe she's been taken to the Sanctuary?"

For all we knew, Corrine was still mysteriously absent from

The Shade. But it was possible that Vivienne had been taken there to be tended by other witches.

We descended from the treehouse and ran back through the woods toward the witch's residence. We bumped into Rose and Caleb, who followed us to the Sanctuary.

When we arrived outside the door, my spine tingled as my ears caught the crying of an infant. Sofia gasped.

"Oh, my God, it's happened already!" Rose exclaimed.

Worries about my son momentarily drifted into the background as excitement overtook me. I forced open the front door, too impatient to wait for somebody to come to answer it, and barged into the entrance hall. We hurried toward the crying, stopping outside one of the bedrooms.

"Vivienne?" I spoke up, a slight tremble in my voice.

The door flung open a moment later, and we found ourselves standing face to face with Corrine. Her thick brown locks were wrapped tightly above her head in a bun, beads of perspiration shining in the roots of her hair.

Her eyes widened, and a look of relief washed over her face. "Oh, thank goodness you're back. Come in! Come in!"

We rushed in to find Vivienne lying on a double bed, cradling a blanket-clad baby in her arms. Xavier sat next to her on the bed. Vivienne looked drained and exhausted, but both of the new parents were positively glowing with happiness.

My throat tightened. My voice choked up, and I could hardly even greet them. I broke out into a smile, joy billowing up within me.

I hurried to Vivienne's bedside and kissed her forehead while looking down at her beautiful baby.

"A boy or a girl?" Sofia asked, arriving by my side along with Rose.

"A girl," Vivienne replied, tears moistening the corners of her eyes as she gazed at her baby.

"How late are we?" Rose asked, smiling at the baby girl.

"A few hours," Xavier replied. His eyes had the same glistening quality as his wife's. They both looked in a daze, lost in their own little bubble with their new child.

Vivienne raised the baby from her chest and handed her to me. I held her in my arms, taking in her features. Fine strands of dark hair covered her head and her eyes were bright blue, closer to my mother's—and my—eye color than to Vivienne or Xavier's. I dipped down and planted a kiss on her tiny nose.

"So you've named her Aurora?" I asked.

"We thought that's what we'd name her... Xavier and I decided on that name months ago if we had a girl. But when she came out and I looked into her eyes for the first time... I wanted to name her after our mother, Derek." Vivienne's eyes shimmered with melancholy even as she smiled. "Victoria."

Victoria Vaughn.

We had lost our mother hundreds of years ago. Her death—caused by a vampire—had been the catalyst to my becoming a hunter before my siblings and I were eventually turned into vampires. My mother had died so long ago that she was but a distant memory. I had been only a teenager in human years, and so for the vast majority of my life, she had been absent.

But the look in my twin sister's eyes stirred up memories of Victoria Lisette Novak. Memories of a beautiful, strong, dutiful woman. A woman my father Gregor Novak hadn't deserved. I wished that she could be here now, that she could hold her new granddaughter in her arms and remark on how similar their eye colors were.

"I'm glad," Rose said, her voice breaking through the haze of my memory. "I prefer the name Victoria."

My daughter was standing several feet away from me, behind Caleb. I had sensed her take a step back as I'd picked up the baby, and now she had moved to the furthest end of the room, where she stood watching the scene. She was wise to do that. Although she'd made great progress in controlling her bloodlust, she still hadn't been a vampire for long, and the blood of babies was particularly sweet.

I placed Victoria into Sofia's ready arms, giving her a chance to greet her niece. Sofia kissed her puffy cheeks and stood with her a while before handing her back to Vivienne. My sister readjusted the blanket before resting Victoria against her chest.

We moved from the bedside and took seats around the room just as someone knocked on the door. Rose, being closest to the door, pulled it open to reveal Aiden standing in the doorway. He held a bouquet of bright yellow sunflowers. He'd come better prepared than us.

"Congratulations," he exclaimed. Corrine took the flowers from Aiden and arranged them in a vase on Vivienne's bedside table while my father-in-law approached the bed. He gestured to the flowers. "I didn't know if I'd find you with a boy or a girl, so I opted for a neutral color."

"Thank you." Vivienne grinned, allowing Aiden to greet the newest member of our family.

"So how has everything been since we've been away?" I asked.

Xavier tore his eyes away from Victoria to face me. "Other than the arrival of Victoria, quite uneventful."

"What happened with you?" Vivienne asked anxiously.

I didn't want to bring up the news of Benjamin now. Not on one of the happiest days of my sister's life.

"It was... eventful," I muttered.

"Well, did you manage to reclaim Ben or not? Where is he?" Vivienne pressed.

I was relieved when Corrine came to my rescue.

"Vivienne," she said, her voice taking on the tone of a scolding schoolteacher as she eyed my sister sternly. "As your midwife, I insist that you keep your focus on your baby and on your recovery. No other topic shall be discussed in this room until you're fully recovered and strong enough to move back into your penthouse with Victoria. Okay?"

Vivienne was clearly not "okay" with it, but Corrine had a way of speaking with finality and my twin didn't argue. She just pursed her lips and nodded reluctantly, while her eyes remained on me, silently pleading for more information about our trip.

Corrine turned to Sofia and me. "I'd like to have a private word with you two," she said. Her expression had turned stony.

Aiden, Rose and Caleb remained in the room while Sofia and I followed Corrine out of the door. She led us along the hallway and into a sitting room. She made sure the door was shut before joining us in the center of the room. Clearly, she didn't want to run any risk of Vivienne overhearing, even with Vivienne's weaker human ears.

What exactly is so secret? My stomach tensed as I took a seat on the couch with Sofia while Corrine began to pace up and down on the rug in front of us.

"What happened to you, Corrine?" Sofia asked. "We were

looking everywhere for you on the island, and then it occurred to us that you might've gotten trapped in The Oasis."

"I was trapped in The Oasis. And if it weren't for River taking compassion on a poor dove locked in a cage, I would likely still be there."

"They turned you into a bird like the other witches?" Sofia asked. "How long have you been back?"

"I believe I returned the same day you left. We just missed each other. I returned with River because Benjamin requested it. We would have stayed with him, but he insisted."

I leaned forward in my seat. "What's happening with him?"

"He…" Corrine drew in a deep breath, clasping her hands together. "He discovered something about himself. He went to visit an oracle and… Oh, God. I hate to be the one to break this news to you… Ben was marked by an Elder as a newborn, and has been bonded with him ever since."

Even though Nuriya had already revealed this to Sofia and me, my breath still hitched to hear it again, this time from Corrine's lips. It made the situation seem that much more real. That much more inescapable.

"We know, Corrine," Sofia said quietly.

The witch's eyebrows shot toward her hairline. "What? How?"

Sofia glanced my way before beginning to recount to Corrine everything that had happened to us since we left. From the meeting with the Drizans, to the storming of The Oasis, to the eventual discovery of what had happened to our son and how we had just made things so much worse for him.

Corrine sank into an armchair. "Oh, no. I had a bad feeling all along about you leaving to break the jinn's bond before I had a chance to talk to you. Even despite them keeping Ben as a prisoner, I'd seen how the Nasiris were helping him, and God knows that boy needs help."

"But what now?" Sofia asked, her voice strained. "What can we possibly do to help my son? Nuriya said that without a second jinni, he won't have enough protection to stop the Elder from luring him back to Cruor." Her voice cracked and trailed off into a sob.

Corrine gazed at us with sad eyes. "For all my years' worth of knowledge, I don't know, honey. I just don't know. I've already discussed the situation in depth with Ibrahim, and he's just as clueless." She paused, and leaned forward to lay a hand on Sofia's knee. Corrine glanced from my wife to me. "You know, the last words Ben spoke to me before I left The Oasis with River were that this was a journey he had to go on alone. Perhaps he was right. You two instigating the Drizans to damage the Nasiris' protection of Ben, perhaps that was like… an arrangement of destiny. Maybe he really is supposed to go through this alone."

I clenched my jaw. In my mind, the question wasn't whether or not this was his destiny. The question was, could my son survive this on his own?

But whatever the answer was, in a sense it didn't matter. Each time we tried to help our son, it only ever seemed to backfire. He was worse off now than before our "help". Maybe Corrine was right. Maybe we just needed to accept that this journey was one Ben had to make alone.

Chapter 5: Ben

I lowered myself closer to the ocean and began to run. I was weightless, floating. Even though my legs moved, my feet grazing the surface of the waves, they merely passed through them. It was as though I hurtled forward by sheer willpower alone. As I picked up speed, I realized that I traveled faster than I had when I'd been a vampire, for I no longer had a physical body to carry along with me.

The sun burst through the clouds overhead. Its rays fell upon me, and I instinctively braced myself to feel the pain, but of course, I felt nothing. The shafts of sunlight shone right through my form, beaming down and making the waves beneath me glisten.

Now that it could no longer harm me, I yearned to feel the sun's warmth on my skin. I could hardly remember what it felt like as a human. And the sea spray that showered over me, I yearned to feel its coolness and smell the salt. Of course, I couldn't. It seemed that the only senses that worked were my hearing and vision—although even my sight was different than it was before. I could see things clearly, yet the world surrounding me appeared washed out, its vibrant colors dulled and faded, like a watercolor painting left out in the sun.

Surging ahead, I still wasn't sure where I should go. I just knew that I couldn't stay in Cruor forever.

Now that I was no longer a threat to my family, perhaps I could find a gate and make my way back to The Shade. But how would I find a gate? When Aisha had first led me into the supernatural dimension, we'd come through a portal in a strange, black desert. Aisha hadn't told me which land that was, so I had no idea how to return there.

Aisha. What had happened to that jinni? Was she in that box still, perhaps back on Julie's ship? I wondered where Julie was now. I was oblivious to how much time had passed since Julie had abandoned me in Cruor. But if the ship was being pulled by sea creatures who were even half as fast as the dolphins and sharks I'd had experience with since being here, I was sure that they would be far away by now.

I recalled the hours before I'd found myself in Cruor. We had boarded Julie's ship, which had been floating near The Tavern. I didn't know how long it'd taken to travel from The Tavern to Cruor because I'd been unconscious for much of the time. But something told me that if I made it to The Tavern, I would have a better chance of making it back to The Shade. There were many wanderers who passed by, and if I just listened in to conversations long enough, perhaps I would catch mention of a gate. Perhaps I might even be able to follow them to it, if the right person came along.

But how on earth did I find The Tavern? I hadn't even the first clue as to which direction to head in. Right now I was just running straight ahead, with no idea where I might end up.

The past weeks merged together in a blur of urgency to solve my mystery. It took a while for it to sink in that I didn't have that problem anymore. I had time now. I was no longer a ticking time bomb. There was no hunger in my stomach, and I wasn't affected by the time of day. I doubted that I would even tire of traveling. As much as I wanted to return to my home to check that everyone I loved was all right, time wasn't the issue it had once been.

And so I kept running, away from the land of the Elders, deeper and deeper into the ocean. By the time the sun set, I still hadn't come across land. I wondered if I'd taken completely the wrong direction, but the increasing frequency of ships that I spotted sailing toward me gave me hope that there were shores nearby.

As night fell, I spotted the outline of an island far to the east. It was some distance away yet, but at least I'd found it. As I moved toward it, I caught sight of something that arrested me. A ship, perhaps three miles in front of me, also moving toward the island. Even from this distance, something about it struck me as familiar. From its size, shape, and the color of its sails, the closer I got to the vessel, the more certain I became that it was Julie's ship. Whether it belonged to her father, I wasn't sure anymore. For all I knew, she didn't even have a father.

It surprised me that Julie would be headed back toward this area. And from the looks of it, she was intending to arrive at the harbor. The ship was on a direct course toward the shipyard, showing no signs of slowing down. Skimming along the waves beside it, I caught up with the ship. Jumping upward, I soared through the air and landed noiselessly on the deck.

When I cast my eyes around, it was clear that something wasn't right. The floorboards were stained with blood. There was splintered wood scattered about, the canvas fabric of the lower sails was torn, and a table had been upturned and ripped apart. The trap door leading down to the lower decks had been ripped from its hinges.

What happened here?

There was nobody navigating the ship, yet the vessel continued speeding ahead. I swept my eyes once more over the deck. Thick reins hung down over the bow of the boat and had been fastened to a mast. Whatever sea creatures served as the engine of this ship were leading it forward of their own volition.

I approached the open trapdoor. Descending the narrow staircase, I found myself at the end of a long, dim corridor that connected all the numerous cabins on this lower deck.

"Julie?" I found myself calling, my voice echoing in my ears.

No reply.

I moved further down the corridor, looking into the first room on my left. Like the deck above, this cabin also looked distressed. Bloodstains tainted the floor and walls, and the door was wrecked. It looked like someone had punched a fist through the wood.

The corridor wound to the right. As I turned the corner, my eyes were drawn to the ceiling.

Three naked figures—men?—were hanging from it. I moved closer, gaping up at their starkly pale skin, hairless heads, and emaciated limbs. I couldn't make out their faces, only the backs of their heads, but as I walked directly underneath them, I caught a glimpse of their hands and feet, stretched out and gripping the walls on either side of them. Gnarled claws extended from their fingers, and their white cuticles were stained with red.

Although nothing could injure me anymore, I felt hesitant to move any closer to them. They were just so… strange. What were they exactly? Apparently yet another species of supernatural creatures to blow my mind. But what were they doing on Julie's ship? And the blood staining their fingers… could that be Julie's blood and that of her companions? Perhaps these creatures had hijacked their ship as they'd navigated away from Cruor.

I backed away from the pale creatures clinging to the ceiling, and cleared my throat. "What are you?" I spoke up.

They remained still, silent and barely breathing—as though I hadn't spoken at all.

I backed further away from them, deciding to abandon my curiosity about them and focus on finding the box I feared Aisha was still trapped in. It was nowhere to be found on this level, so I took the staircase down to the deck beneath.

The last I'd seen of the box had been on the rocks beneath the mountain where I'd encountered Basilius. As a spirit I'd roamed that whole area during the time it had taken me to build up courage to abandon my physical form on the cliffside. I would've noticed the box if they'd left it there. So I could only assume that they'd carried it back to their ship. And as it turned out, I was right. Moving from room to room, I discovered the white oblong box in a small storage room near the galley.

I lowered my hands over the lid of the box. They didn't pass through it, as my form did with other hard objects. Instead, I felt resistance, the same kind of resistance I'd felt while pressing my hands against The Oasis' invisible barrier. I found myself relishing the illusion of solid contact. The feeling of touching something gave me a sense of grounding. I continued to press my palms down against it for several moments before calling, "Aisha?"

There came no reply. My hands instinctively roamed down the side of the box, searching for the lid's ridge. The box was locked with a padlock, but as I moved to grab hold of it, my fingers passed right through it. I could feel resistance with the box's surface itself, however. Did I have any strength to force the lid open? I curled my fingers around the curve of the lid and tried to heave upward, but the effort caused my feet to sink into the floor.

Even if I was able to stand on a solid surface, this box was clearly magical. I doubted that anything but its key could open it.

"Are you in there, Aisha?" I asked again.

I cursed in frustration. It was torturous to be less than a

foot away from the jinni and yet completely unable to help her. *What do I do now?* I was certain that Aisha was in the box. I couldn't imagine for the life of me what reason Julie and her companions would have for releasing her—they would know full well that Aisha would unleash her wrath on them the moment she got free. Aisha had already threatened Julie's life once back on the island where we met Arron, and I'd seen how shaken the vampire was by her.

I'd stopped Aisha from murdering Julie that day. Now I thought bitterly to myself that I should have just let the jinni drive a knife through her.

I heaved a sigh, staring down at the stubborn box. *There's nothing I can do to open this.* I just had to hope that somehow Aisha would find a way out. If she did manage that, I wouldn't worry about her. She was powerful and she would be able to find her way back home… although after what Bahir had said about Nuriya being in grave danger, and Aisha having feared The Oasis was under attack, I wasn't sure what kind of home she'd return to.

Whatever the case, my hovering over this box any longer wasn't going to help her. I stood up and was about to leave the room when I caught sight of a mirror hanging directly in front of me. Yet as I stared into it, my reflection didn't stare back. All I could see was the empty wall behind me.

I'd become invisible. And, given the lack of movement

from those creatures out in the hallway when I had spoken, I suspected that I was inaudible to the outside world, too.

I staggered backward, half of my back disappearing into the wall, my eyes still locked on the mirror.

It's like I don't exist.

I didn't know what I'd been expecting—that ghosts were visible to people? I hadn't thought much about it. Now I realized that even if I made it back to The Shade, nobody would even know. They couldn't see or hear me, I couldn't touch them... heck, I couldn't even pick up a pen and write them a note. I was trapped in this... half-existence.

I would be nothing but a shadow, roaming the woods, trying to reconnect with my former life. It took a while for the notion to fully sink in.

But still, I needed to return to The Shade. Even if I couldn't communicate with them, I needed to know that everyone was all right, if only for my peace of mind. Besides, that island was my home. If I didn't return there, where would I go?

Pulling myself together, I tore my eyes away from the empty mirror and moved back out into the hallway. I climbed back up the staircase, intending to return to the upper deck, but on arriving at the level beneath, I found myself face to face with one of the ceiling-hanging creatures, all the more alarming now that it stood directly in front of me.

For the first time, I took in its face. Its lips were withered and two long, razor-sharp fangs—sharper than I'd ever seen in a vampire—protruded from its mouth. Its nose was partially receded into its skull. It was staring straight at me, or rather, straight through me. It lurched suddenly, and although my instinct was to duck, I should've remembered that there was no need. It passed right through me, as though I was nothing but a cloud of mist, and continued down the corridor. Its movement was strange. It almost shuffled, as though it had injured one leg, and yet it possessed an alarming speed and agility.

I'd never seen any creature like this before. Certain features reminded me of vampires—like its fangs, claws, and pale skin—yet it was like no vampire I'd ever seen.

Shuffling came from my left, and I turned around to see another creature moving toward me. It appeared to be in a hurry and whizzed right through me, followed shortly by a third creature. They scurried to the end of the corridor and raced up the stairs toward the upper deck.

I wasn't sure where they were going or what they intended to do. But there was nothing else I could accomplish by staying on this boat. It seemed that Aisha would remain trapped here until fate decided to free her.

I followed the creatures to the upper deck, where I found all three standing near the bow of the boat. One of them had taken the reins and was apparently slowing the animals to a stop. Looking around, I realized that we had already reached the harbor.

I didn't know what the trio wanted to do in The Tavern—perhaps stop over for the night and rest until morning. Somehow, I found it hard to imagine them booking a room in the Blue Tavern's guesthouse. For that matter, they didn't appear to be the type of creature that would be welcome in The Tavern at all.

Pushing aside thoughts of them, I floated off the ship and drifted down toward the moonlit shipyard. I turned my mind to thinking about how exactly I was going to glean information about the nearest gate.

Heading to the pub ought to be my first option. That was the hub of this island, where most travelers passed through. In theory I could just hover around there for as long as it took to overhear something.

When I arrived outside the building, it was packed, as it always seemed to be. Although I hardly needed to worry about finding a seat anymore—which was a good thing, for there were none. I wandered around the tables, getting as close to the patrons as I wanted, and listened to their conversations. I saw no familiar faces other than the man tending the bar. He'd been here the night I'd arrived in the guest house, the same night I'd met Julie.

As I glanced over to the same table where I'd first spoken with her, a memory flooded back to me. That same night, sitting around the table next to us, had been four hooded vampires. I hadn't paid attention to their faces much, and now I wondered if they had been the same four companions who had accosted me on Julie's ship.

I shook away the memory. It didn't matter anymore, anyway. Whatever Julie had been thinking, however long she had been planning her deception… it was all irrelevant now.

I continued drifting slowly around the pub, moving from table to table, until morning arrived and the crowd began to thin a little. So far, I hadn't heard anything that could help me. Most who'd sat in the pub that night seemed to be wanderers, and although they'd spoken of recent travels, none mentioned a voyage to the human realm.

It was so bizarre to be here in this supernatural world, a world that only a tiny fraction of the human population was even aware of. I should have been fascinated by these creatures' tales, and yet once I'd realized a conversation wouldn't lead to the information I sought, it faded into the background, mundane and uninteresting.

All I wanted now was to return home. It was what my soul ached for, even though I'd already had premonitions of how painful it would be.

Chapter 6: Ben

I waited all day in the pub, listening to the conversations of the myriad of supernatural species coming in and out, until evening arrived. Now that it was more crowded again, I stood up to avoid someone coming over to my bench and sitting right on top of me. I settled into the same routine as the night before, wandering about the tables, listening and trying to catch hint of a traveler who might be intending to pass through a gate.

It was toward the end of the night, having still had no luck in overhearing mention of a gate, that I decided to leave this room and head upstairs, toward the bedrooms. Since the crowds were thinning from this place anyway, perhaps I might overhear some useful information in the guest rooms above, like comrades discussing plans before they drifted off.

I headed toward the exit and reached for the door handle before my hand just sank right into it. Straightening, I stared at the door in front of me before walking headfirst into it. I winced a little, half expecting my etherealness to disappear just as my head made contact with the wood. But I sank through it, emerging on the other side, at the bottom of the staircase leading up to the guest rooms. The staircase I'd climbed only days ago with Julie.

I drifted higher and higher until I arrived at the very top floor. I figured that I could start wandering around here and then make my way down to the lower levels.

To my right was a large window—the same one I'd taken refuge at to get away from the scent of human blood. I looked out through the glass, able to see the ocean beyond the high wall that surrounded the island. The window was closed, but judging from how the trees were swaying, there was a gentle breeze. I wished that I could feel the wind on my face right then.

Tearing my eyes away from the window, I turned around. Then I stopped in my tracks. Someone was slumped on the floor at the opposite end of the hallway. A man with a long, bushy gray beard, his eyes closed. His head hung over his chest, as though he'd fallen asleep while sitting… or was dead.

Wrapped around him was a tattered brown cloak. I wasn't sure what creature this was exactly—a vampire, a human, or perhaps something else—but whatever he was, he looked like a tramp.

As I approached him, his head shot up suddenly. I was alarmed to find his faded brown eyes on me. I gaped at him, speechless. He could… see me?

Now that I was closer, his skin was of the same quality as mine, pale, ethereal and slightly translucent.

He didn't look surprised to see me. He just looked me over from head to toe with mild interest before rolling his head back down and resuming his previous position.

"Can you hear me?" I found myself asking.

He grunted. "Yes, boy," he said, his voice deep and thick with slumber.

Keeping a distance of a couple of feet between us, I bent down to his level. "Who are you?" I asked. "And what are you doing here?"

"I could ask the same of you," he mumbled.

Coming across another ghost was something I hadn't expected. I'd no idea who this stranger was, but somehow it was comforting to meet someone who was in the same position as me, and had likely been in it much longer. It was like coming across a compatriot in a foreign land.

Slowly, he turned his eyes on me again. They looked

heavy, as though it was a struggle to lift them halfway.

It hadn't occurred to me that ghosts needed sleep. I hadn't felt any need for it, just as I no longer felt hunger… or anything, for that matter.

"You disturb me, boy," he said, irritation now crossing his face.

"I apologize," I said. "I only recently left my body, and I have questions."

He pursed his lips, his jowls trembling slightly beneath his beard.

"What exactly do you want with me?" he asked, eyes narrowing.

"I'm seeking the location of gates leading to the human realm," I replied. "That's where I have come from, and that's where my home is."

Even up close to him, it was hard for me to say exactly what body he had once possessed before he became a spirit—ghosts were already so pale—but I guessed from the formation of his upper jaw that he had been a vampire.

The old man's eyes drooped closed, and his head lolled once again.

"Is there any way that you could help me?" I asked, increased urgency in my tone.

"Hush!" he said. "You'll scare away the dreams."

My brows knotted. "Dreams?"

"I'd almost caught one! Just sit down and close your eyes." He paused, waiting for me to slide down to the floor next to him, before continuing, "I will show you how to catch dreams. It is very easy. All it requires is for you to extend your mind..."

I looked at the man in bemusement. I realized that I hadn't tried to close my eyes since leaving my body. For that matter, I couldn't even remember if I had been blinking.

"Relax your head, and close your eyes," the man commanded me again.

Assuming the same slumped position as him, I lowered my head downward and closed my eyes. There was just darkness. Which in itself was surprising. I'd expected that perhaps I would see right through the thin walls of my eyelids.

I was really in no mood for whatever game this ghost was proposing, but I didn't know when or if I would come across another person who could hear and see me—another ghost. I didn't see what other option I had but to pander to him in the hope that he'd be more likely to help me out afterward.

"I'm not sure what I'm supposed to be seeing," I muttered. "I see nothing."

The man breathed out impatiently. "You try too hard. Just loosen your mind and wait... the next one will come soon."

I didn't understand him, but I humored him all the same. I kept my eyes closed, and tried to "loosen my mind"...

whatever that meant.

And then I saw something. A warm golden light trickled into my mind's eye. A scene began to form, slowly, as if being painted in with brushstrokes, until I found myself beholding a beach. A beautiful white-sand beach. A glowing orange sun hung over the horizon, already halfway down in its descent. The shore was empty except for a couple walking hand in hand with the waves lapping around their ankles. The woman wore a wedding gown, while the man was dressed in a smart black tuxedo.

Then the sky darkened, as if God Himself had flicked a light switch. There was no moon or stars in the sky and the only light seemed to be emanating from the sea. It had turned a bright green, almost neon color, and it glowed eerily. Heads of seven giant serpents reared from the water, hissing and flashing white fangs. The couple were fixed to the spot, too stunned to duck out of the way before—

"No, no!" The old man's gruff voice shattered the vision. I opened my eyes. He was shaking his head angrily. "That was a black dream! We don't want to live in those. Close your eyes again and we'll search for a good one."

A black dream, I thought to myself as I closed my eyes again. *A nightmare. So, somehow, ghosts are able to intercept dreams.* Yet another new thing I'd learned about this spirit existence.

We weren't waiting as long for the next vision. It emerged quickly in my mind. A beautiful poppy-scattered meadow, through which ran a pure white horse, ridden by… an ogre—the smallest ogre I had ever seen. It must have been a child. A boy. He wore a shiny metal chest plate and a gem-studded helmet, and strapped to his short, chubby legs were silver knee guards. A sword dangled from his belt—a sword so large it was almost as tall as him. He rode across the meadow with practiced grace, then guided the steed into a forest. They whipped through the trees until they reached a clearing, at the end of which lay a steep drop.

Even as the horse approached the edge of the cliff, still the child didn't slow it down. If anything the steed sped up. And then, with one giant leap, the horse launched off the cliff into a terrifying freefall. The boy's hands dug into his steed's neck, and just as the two were about to collide with the rocks at the bottom of the cliff, a pair of magnificent wings sprouted from the horse's back. Wings that beat hard and fast until the horse soared with the ogre high in the clear blue sky. The child gasped with pleasure as he beheld an entire world sprawled out beneath him—trees, lakes, hills…

I opened my eyes and shook my head.

Enough of this.

I looked at the old man. His eyes were still closed, and his face was… almost unrecognizable. His sour, scowling demeanor had vanished, and his face had lit up. He swayed gently from side to side, as if hypnotized, so taken by the fantasy of some ogre child sleeping within one of the rooms of the guest house.

I needed to interrupt him, but I felt almost bad to burst the bubble of happiness this otherwise miserable man appeared to be in. I wondered whether he lived in The Tavern. Whether he haunted this guesthouse corridor every day.

"I'm sorry," I said. "I'll leave you alone, if you'll just answer a question."

He grunted in frustration and when he opened his eyes, his face had resumed its former grumpy look.

"That was a good one!" he fumed, his lips curling. "It's been three days since I roamed a dream as good as that!"

"I'm sorry," I repeated. "I wish to leave you alone, as I said. Answer my question, and you can return to the dream."

"What do you want?" he snapped.

"I'm looking for a gate that will lead me into the human realm. Do you have any idea how I might find one?"

The man's mouth formed in a hard line, his brows furrowed as he continued glaring up at me. "Hm. There are some ogres who may be able to take you there," he mumbled.

"Ogres? Which ogres?"

"The ogres who guard the walls of this island. They

discovered a gate some miles away and they frequent it together to gather food for themselves. Humans."

"How do you know this?" I asked.

He smiled bitterly at me, and there was a trace of melancholy in his jaded eyes. "When you haunt an island for six hundred years, you know things like this."

Six hundred years. He's lived this way for six hundred years.

The thought threw me off, and it took my brain a few seconds to form my next question. "And, uh, do you know the names of the ogres I need to seek out?"

"Just look for Rufus," he said. "They usually travel in his ship."

"And do you know how often they go?"

"This is more than one question," he said, a pained look on his face. "I don't know how long that dream is going to last, or even that I'll be able to walk in it again after you scared it off!"

"How often do the ogres go to the human realm?" I insisted, even though I felt bad for it. But I'd realized by now that I had the power to interrupt his pleasure, and unless he gave me what I wanted, there was no reason for me to go away.

"Usually twice a week," he murmured. "At least."

"Thank you," I said. Finally I motioned to turn around, but something kept me rooted to the spot, staring down at the old man curled up on the floor. "May I have your name?"

"Ernest," he growled. "Now, shoo!"

"Thank you, Ernest," I replied.

He flicked a hand at me before clamping his eyes shut again. His face scrunched up in concentration, and then, after a few moments, relaxed. The lines in his face smoothed and his expression returned to one of deep peace. I guessed he'd managed to re-immerse himself in the same child's fantasy. Or perhaps this night had been a lucky one, and he'd found two happy places to lose his aching soul in.

Chapter 7: Ben

Rufus the ogre. Ernest had said that he was one of the guards on the island. So, abandoning the guest house, I headed straight for the wall that surrounded The Tavern. I recalled the door that Julie had led me through. An ogre had been positioned there. I managed to find my way back to that same spot, where, no surprise, I found an ogre, though not the same one as before.

He was alone, however. Which meant that in order to find out anything about him, I had to hover near him, waiting for him to have an interaction with someone. Finally, a werewolf approached the door, requesting to be let outside onto the beach. He addressed the ogre as Hector. At least now I'd learned he wasn't Rufus. Ogres, however, seemed to be in the minority on this island and I guessed that they would get together to eat. So I waited with Hector.

Once the sun peeked over the horizon, Hector left his post and headed out toward the beach. I soon caught sight of where he was heading—to a group of ogres sitting around a fire. As we approached, I learned that one of them—a particularly large and hideous-looking one—went by the name of Rufus. In that very conversation, they spoke of their last venture into the human realm. How they had managed to swipe a group of six humans from a mountain range—mountain climbers, I assumed. They were planning to go again in two days' time.

So from then on, it became a waiting game. I stuck by Rufus's side the whole time, even returning to his cave while he slept.

Finally, the evening arrived and Rufus gathered near the harbor with the other ogres. They boarded a large ship pulled by five giant grey sharks and set off. Hovering near the stern of the vessel, I watched The Tavern fading into the distance and eavesdropped on the ogres' conversation. All of them were talking animatedly about what ghastly meal they would cook up once they'd gathered their humans, and were already arguing over what the main course should be served with. I was both amazed and sickened by just how long they were able to talk about the subject of food and the tiniest details they went into. As a ghost, I couldn't seem to block out my hearing, and thus had no means of escape from their stomach-turning discussion of the butchery process.

I let out a deep sigh of relief when a small—apparently uninhabited—island came into view. It reminded me a little of the islet where Aisha had taken me to meet Arron for the first time after she had collected him from Aviary. I guessed that this one was probably in a similar area, because we had not been traveling long.

The excitement rising in the ogres was practically palpable as they trundled off the boat and began hurrying onto the island. They tramped through the undergrowth, bashing aside the occasional tree with their mighty elbows. I followed and hovered above them, trying to see exactly where they were headed. Eventually, I spotted it. Surrounded by slabs of rock was a wide black hole, the depths of which were speckled with sparkling stars.

I waited as, one by one, the ogres tumbled through—many of them letting out bellows as the vacuum consumed them.

After the last ogre had disappeared through the gate, I approached it. My last experience jumping through one of these had been as a vampire, and a suction had pulled me down. Now, I couldn't feel any pull at all. It seemed that the vacuum had no effect on me. I entered the hole and had to travel down it by the force of my own will. For the first time, I was able to see the inside of this crater without being rushed down at eye watering speed. Although, frankly, there wasn't a lot to see, apart from the strange, swirling blue smoke that formed the walls of the tunnel and the apparent night sky beyond it.

I wondered for a moment what would happen if I drifted through the wall. If I could even drift through it. This strange starry sky that appeared to surround us, what was that exactly? I guessed with my subtle body, I probably could pass through the tunnel walls, but I'd no idea what might happen, and I didn't want to risk finding out.

Instead I focused my gaze directly downward and sped up, until eventually a light shone through the other end and I emerged on the other side. Surrounding me was a world of white mountains. I was standing on a staggeringly high cliff. I wondered where I was exactly. I would have to travel until I found some human habitation where I could figure out where in the world I was. I wasn't sure which direction to start in. I looked around for the ogres and spotted their large footprints in the snow, trailing down over the edge of the peak. *Following them would be a good bet.*

CHAPTER 8: RIVER

My brother, Jamil, walked by my side as we ambled along the dark beach. My sisters played in the waves, while my mother watched over them.

I drew in a deep breath of fresh ocean air.

Since returning to The Shade without Ben, I'd woken up every day with the hope that, somehow, he would find a loophole and return to us. However irrational it was, holding on to this hope was what got me through each day. The chilling words the oracle had spoken to me that day in her cave still haunted me: *"Very soon this man may not be the same one you fell for."* But I tried to stop thinking about where Ben could be now, or what state he might be in.

Ben's parents had recently returned to the island, but I hadn't gotten a chance to speak to them yet. They'd been busy of course, what with Vivienne giving birth. I didn't want to bother them yet to find out what had happened on their journey with the dragons. After all that had been revealed by Hortencia regarding Ben's connection with the Elder, I couldn't help but feel that breaking the jinn's bond now wasn't a good idea. Corrine felt the same way, but unfortunately, Derek and Sofia had left before we'd had a chance to explain Ben's predicament. As crazy as it was, the eternal bond Ben had formed with the Nasiris was the least of his worries, and might be the one thing that was protecting him.

I wasn't sure if Corrine had filled them in by now, but I was anxious to find out the result of their excursion. I decided to wait another day before speaking to them. The truth was, I was afraid that I wouldn't be able to keep my voice from breaking while talking to them. Especially to Sofia. I'd promised her that I would stay with Ben and help him find a solution.

Since I'd returned, I'd stayed with my family. I'd answered their many questions, including why I was so cold, and recounted what had happened to me before I came across them in The Oasis. Although I'd revealed most things to my mother, I refused to go into detail about what happened to

Ben and exactly why I had returned. It was too raw. I just gave her a truthful summary—that although I'd wanted to stay with Ben to help him, as I'd promised that I would, he hadn't wanted to put me in danger and so he'd sent me back with Corrine. I was glad that my mother didn't press for more details. I wasn't ready to talk about them. I doubted I would be for a long time.

Telling them that I was a half-blood sent my mother into hysterics. We'd been staying on this island for days now, but she was still struggling to accept the situation. It was as though she half expected this all to be some kind of elaborate prank. The strange creatures surrounding us were just costumed actors who would leap out of their highly realistic fake skin any second. There wasn't really a spell of night over this place, since witches weren't real, and someone had simply erected some giant covering that looked… exactly like the night sky?

Her convoluted theories were crazier than just accepting the situation for what it was. And, in fact, I knew that she couldn't really believe her doubts—she'd seen too much already. She was just clinging to them as a way of coping with her reality being turned on its head. I was just waiting for her to say out loud that yes, supernaturals existed, and we were living on an island full of them.

We stayed with Anna and Kyle for the first few days. They

treated us like family. They had three children of their own, and the older two had already been turned into vampires. Still, they cleared out two rooms for us and made our stay as comfortable as they possibly could. None of us wanted to be a burden on them any longer, and Anna found us a three-bedroom townhouse that wasn't being occupied just a few streets away from theirs. So we'd recently moved there.

My mother talked of returning to New York, but I told her that I couldn't return, at least not now. First of all, I was still a half-blood and there was no cure for me yet on the horizon, and secondly, even if I could leave The Shade… it would feel like cutting off any connection I had left with Ben. This was his home. His world. As unceremoniously as I had been thrust into this world of supernaturals, I was a part of it now. Even if we found a cure for me, I simply couldn't imagine going back to my life in New York. I could never see things the same again, nor simply resume the life I'd had like nothing had ever happened.

Although there was much talk of supernaturals of late—especially after the footage that had been broadcast by the media—like my mother, and indeed like I had been, most of the population was still living in denial. If I were to ever speak to anyone about what I'd witnessed, I'd be deemed crazy.

Of course, my mother wouldn't return without me, and so we all found ourselves staying here in The Shade. My sisters found the place both wondrous and terrifying, but they were much quicker to adjust to their concept of the universe being blown apart than my mother. Jamil, on the other hand... never mind all this crazy supernatural stuff, he was still acclimating to being able to walk on his own two feet, being able to talk and perform the most basic functions that we all took for granted. We were all still getting used to this new life of his.

One of the countless things he had asked us about was our father, and my mother told him the truth—in front of Dafne, too. My mother told him our father's downward spiral leading to imprisonment had been many years in the making. Jamil was surprisingly accepting of it. He said that he had been aware of our father not being around much, even if his symptoms had been so severe that he couldn't quite form the conclusion as a coherent thought.

I looked at him now as he stood next to me, his face turned toward the ocean, his brow slightly furrowed. I slid my hand into his and squeezed it. He was still like a stranger, to us, and to himself. I hadn't wanted to overburden my family with too much information about supernaturals, but my mother had insisted that I tell her what happened to me.

"How are you feeling?" I asked Jamil, my voice slightly hoarse from underuse.

He nodded slowly, glancing down at me with his dark

eyes. "Okay," he said.

He paused, running his tongue over his lower lip.

"What are you thinking about?" I wondered.

"I… I don't really know," he replied, running a hand through his dark hair. "Everything that I couldn't think before, I guess… I'm honestly not sure what my life was before now. It's almost like it never happened. As though I've just woken up from a long, strange dream. And how I am now was my natural state all along. Like I just needed something to wake me up… am I making any sense?"

I nodded encouragingly. "I understand."

"Thinking back on it now," he continued, "it seems to be a blur of colors, frustration… and Mom."

I smiled, tears creeping into the corners of my eyes. "You know Mom didn't love you any less because you were autistic. She would've continued caring for you for as long as she physically could."

He swallowed, his own eyes moistening. "I know."

My eyes traveled to his lower arm, bare beneath his T-shirt. His tattoo was gone, as was mine, and everyone else's who had returned from The Oasis. This had been part of Ben's deal with the jinn. It was strange to be without the tattoo. I'd had it for such a long time that I'd gotten used to its unpleasantness.

I'd been scared at first that the removal of Jamil's tattoo

could somehow affect the miraculous recovery he was exhibiting. That perhaps, since I was no longer officially part of the Nasiri family, they were no longer interested. They would withdraw this gift from me. Thankfully, the cure that the jinn had given him seemed permanent, unaffected by whether he remained branded by them or whether I remained one of their serfs.

"I feel… excited," my brother murmured, interrupting the silence that had fallen between us. His eyes were filled with wonder as he took in our breathtaking surroundings. "I can walk, talk… heck, even think clearly. It feels like I've entered a new world where anything is possible."

I reached my arms around his neck and pulled his head down so that I could plant a kiss on his cheek. "Anything *is* possible," I whispered, clamping my eyes shut. The words lanced through my heart as they reminded me of the small hope I still clung to that Ben would return to me.

Jamil looked down at me thoughtfully, wiping away my tears with his thumbs. He kissed my forehead. "You really like that boy, don't you?"

I gave him a pained smile. "Yeah," I croaked.

Although I shed silent tears in bed each night, I'd been trying so hard not to break down in front of my family. But with my newfound brother looking down at me, his eyes so similar to my father's, it exacerbated my emotions—the grief I felt over losing Ben—and I couldn't stop myself. I buried my head against my older brother's chest and sobbed.

"Hey," he soothed me, rubbing my back. "It's okay. I'm sure you'll see him again. He's a vampire, right? They're supposed to be immortal?"

I couldn't bring myself to answer, but I appreciated his comforting all the same, no matter how baseless it was.

Screams pierced the air. Jamil and I whirled around to catch sight of our mother and sisters moving frantically toward the shore. Women tended to overreact to creepy-crawlies and slimy things in general, me being guilty of it myself, but from the urgency of their movements, I quickly realized that they had seen something much worse than a hermit crab.

"Mom?" I yelled. "What's wrong?"

I sped up, knowing that I would reach them with my speed before they exited the ocean. Quickly outpacing Jamil even with his long legs, I hurtled toward the waves. Jamil and I had wandered some way up the shore, but it didn't take long for me to come within ten feet of them. I would reach them before they reached dry sand—

My mother took a tumble, and she fell beneath the surface, while my sisters hurried ahead.

"Mom!" I yelled again.

I hurried into the waves and had just about reached her

when, in a blur of red and teal blue, something slimy and heavy shot out from the waves and slapped hard against my face. I lost my footing, staggered back and fell. I shot back up to my feet. My head felt dizzy from the assault. To my horror, I found myself staring down at a blue-tailed mermaid with flaming red hair. Her arms were locked around my mother's neck, causing my mother to struggle and choke for breath as the waves rolled over her. The mermaid tugged on her and began retreating deeper into the ocean.

"No!" I screamed.

I launched myself into the waves and managed to grab hold of my mother's leg before the creature swam out of reach.

"Let go of her!" I hissed at the mermaid. I wasn't sure whether she could even understand me.

It only seemed to anger the creature. She bared a set of razor-sharp black teeth. Teeth that made my skin crawl. One jab of those into my mother's throat could easily end her life.

I had no weapons on me, and, being a half-vampire, no claws or natural defenses with which to defend myself. All I had was my speed. Moving forward as fast as I could, I balled my right hand into a fist and threw a punch square into the mermaid's face.

Part of me expected to miss, but I hit my mark. She loosened her grip on my mother. My mother struggled to keep herself above water as she clutched her throat. She choked on a mouthful of seawater as a wave rolled over her head. I grabbed her by the midriff and began pulling her toward the beach with all the speed I could muster.

Then came a shriek from behind us. The mermaid's shock had subsided and she was gaining speed on us.

I looked desperately toward the shore, where Jamil was moving toward the Port with my sisters, all three of them shouting for help.

We weren't going to reach land in time. The mermaid was simply too fast. *Who is this mermaid?* She didn't look like the one Ben and I had brought in on the submarine—and besides, that one had been badly injured by Shadow. I would have been surprised if she'd even survived a day after the dog's attack. Who, then, was she? As far as I was aware, the two merfolk Ben and I had carried through the boundary were the only ones who'd visited these waters. And wasn't Ibrahim supposed to have gotten rid of the two of them ages ago?

The mermaid caught up with us and once again grabbed hold of my mother. The creature tugged so hard at my mother's ankle, I feared that trying to hold on might dislocate one of her limbs, and to make matters worse, my mother had a weakness in her lower spine. I could see from her eyes how much pain she was in.

The mermaid sensed my hesitation, and with a huge tug,

she managed to pull my mother right out of my grasp. The mermaid's fierce tail writhed as she jolted away. If I hadn't leaped forward and grabbed hold of the tip of it, she would have dragged my mother into deep waters without me.

Although I had no claws, I dug my fingers into her scales as hard as I could, even as the mermaid writhed violently and tried to shake me off. It was like wrestling with a slippery anaconda. I knew I didn't stand a chance for long. My mother's head had been pushed underwater again, if I didn't manage to get to her in time—

Splashes thundered behind me. I cast my eyes over my shoulder just in time to see a giant dog bounding toward us in the waves. I thought for a moment that Shadow had come to the rescue, until I realized that this creature was the wrong color. It wasn't a dog. It was an enormous, shaggy brown wolf.

As my hands slipped from the mermaid's tail, the wolf reached the creature and, opening its heavy jaws, clamped them around the mermaid's midriff. She let out a shriek as blood spilled from her insides and stained the water surrounding us. While the werewolf chomped on the mermaid, I leapt toward my mother. I caught her arm and held her tight, hauling her to the surface. She choked and spluttered, coughing out seawater and drawing in rasping breaths. I wrapped an arm around her waist and kicked my legs hard, propelling us both toward the shore.

"Hurry!" the wolf growled behind us.

I turned back to see that the wolf had let go of the mermaid—who now floated motionless in the water—and was dashing toward us. I was confused as to the wolf's command to hurry, since it seemed that the mermaid was already dead. Then I looked beyond the corpse to see in the distance the ocean swelling. Teal-green tinged the water, a sea of scales shimmering in the moonlight beneath the ocean's surface. Then over two dozen heads poked out of the waves—each sharing the same fearsome features as the mermaid I'd just tackled.

I let out a gasp and kicked harder. The wolf caught up with us. He—or was it a she?—allowed my mother to climb onto his back and carried her the rest of the way to the beach while I hurried after them.

Reaching land, my mother flopped off the werewolf and lay panting on her back on the sand, wheezing and rubbing her throat. I gazed back out toward the ocean to see the crowd of merfolk racing toward the shore.

I glanced at the werewolf, who also looked confused—as confused as a wolf could look.

Where have these merfolk come from? And how on earth did they all gain entrance to The Shade?

CHAPTER 9: DEREK

Since we returned to The Shade, many people had inquired about our journey, so I called a meeting in the Great Dome. Sofia and I arrived in the council hall before the appointed time so that we would have a few minutes of peace before the bombardment of questions started.

As we entered the room and headed toward the raised platform designed for the king and queen to sit upon, I stopped short. The stately chairs Vivienne had designed for Sofia and me were missing. Our raised seats had been built more like thrones than regular chairs. They were large and heavy, and had been sealed into the floor. I moved closer to see that the chairs had been unceremoniously ripped from the stone.

I exchanged glances with Sofia. Her expression was marred with a frown.

"Who would do this?" she whispered.

Throughout all our time of ruling over the island, nothing like this had happened before. Heck, I didn't think that a single chair in this room, even the movable ones surrounding the meeting table, had been taken out. Furniture in this room was to be kept as it was—specifically for the purposes of our council.

Unnerved, I swept my eyes around the room, as if expecting to find the culprit lurking in a shadowy corner. But the Dome was empty, and there were no signs of the chairs anywhere.

There was a knock at the door, which clicked open a second later. Xavier. He'd arrived here early, like us. Dying to find out what happened, he would've left Corrine with Vivienne.

He spotted Sofia's and my missing seats almost immediately.

"Did you do that?" he asked, his face twisting in confusion.

Sofia and I shook our heads. "We just got here and found it like this," Sofia murmured. "We've no idea what happened."

I bent down on the platform, running my hand over the

stumps where the legs of the chairs had been. The splinters of wood pricked my fingers, residue of where the chairs had been fixed.

Of course, missing chairs weren't a big deal. They could easily be replaced. It was the intent of this action that left me ill at ease. If someone had just needed to borrow a couple of chairs, they could have easily taken them from around the table. Ripping these chairs from the floor would render them unusable—they would have been badly damaged in the process. No, whoever took them wasn't interested in chairs. This was a direct affront to Sofia and me. *Who would target us in this way?* I couldn't think of a single person on the island who would do such a thing. The Shade accommodated many residents, the population being far too great for me to know everyone on a personal level, but I liked to think that my people were happy under our rule, and loved and respected the king and queen.

Still shaken, I forced the thought aside and shifted my focus back to Xavier.

"We will need to launch an investigation into who did this," I said, "but for now, I don't want this to distract from our meeting. We already set an agenda and we should stick to it until all questions are answered."

I pulled up one of the lower chairs from around the table and sat down at the same level as the council members. Sofia followed my lead. It wasn't that I was power-hungry and required a special throne to lord it over all my subjects. And neither was Sofia. But when the two of us were leading a conversation, being on a raised platform allowed us to better communicate with a room full of people. We could see each person clearly as they talked, and it aided understanding. Besides, elevated seats were a sign of respect, and there was nothing wrong with that when the respect was genuine. I liked to believe that Sofia and I had done enough to command respect, rather than demand it.

Xavier started asking questions—questions he couldn't ask us back in the Sanctuary because Corrine had forbidden talk of anything but Vivienne's recovery. Even though Xavier knew that the reason I'd called this meeting was to recount everything in one go rather than having to repeat it multiple times to dozens of people, he apparently couldn't help himself. He was too anxious to hear what had happened and why we had returned without Benjamin.

I gave in and started explaining, but I didn't get far before the door opened again and about fifty people piled in, mostly curious vampires and witches—excluding Corrine but including Ibrahim—who had not accompanied us on the excursion. Surprisingly, there were also many present who had come with us. Neither Rose nor Caleb were among them—I assumed they had retired to bed—and the dragons were also notably absent, not that they attended many meetings anyway. They would've returned to their mountain apartments, no doubt eager to be reunited with their lovers.

The newcomers gathered around the table, and surprise registered in some eyes as they noticed Sofia's and my missing seats. Before we could be hit with a wave of questions, I cleared my throat and spoke up, "I don't know what happened here. It is something that I must investigate later."

I was about to begin recounting our voyage when the door blasted open. Saira's huge werewolf form bounded inside and skidded across the floor. Riding on her back were River's two sisters, brother and mother. River entered the room after her. She was soaking wet and shivering.

"Merfolk," she gasped. "There is a whole swarm of them on the beach! One almost kidnapped my mother just now!"

"What?" I breathed. My eyes shot to Ibrahim. "Did you not get rid of those two merfolk Ben and River brought in on the sub?"

"A lot's been going on, Derek," Ibrahim replied. "It's only since you left that I even had an opportunity to see to the task. I got the help of two other witches, but searching the water, we found neither the mermaid nor the merman. I thought that perhaps they'd grown tired of these shores and left the island for deeper waters. Otherwise, they were sneaky enough to avoid our detection. Whatever the case, we were unable to find them."

"There are way more than two now!" River urged. "There's like a whole wave of them, and they were surging toward the island."

"This meeting is postponed." I looked around at the witches present in the Dome. "We must all head to the beach at once. Which beach exactly?"

"Near the Port," River replied, shakily.

"I killed one of them," Saira growled. "It was the quickest way to free River's mother. That seems to have angered them greatly. I haven't the first clue as to what they're doing on this island, but they are not happy. Really not happy."

"My mother cannot walk well," River said, looking anxiously back at Nadia. "Her back was injured in the attack. She needs—"

"Shayla," I called, stalling the short witch as she was about to vanish to the beach with a group of vampires. "Please stay with River's mother and tend to her injury."

Shayla nodded and, leaving the group of vampires, approached Nadia, who was still perched awkwardly on the back of the she-wolf.

"You stay with your mom, River," Sofia said, eyeing the girl. "And here..." She reached around her shoulders and removed her shawl before handing it to River. "You're freezing, put this on."

"Thank you." River looked at her gratefully.

I turned to Ibrahim, who was still standing beside me, waiting for my order. Except for Xavier, the rest of the room had emptied by now, witches having transported everyone to the beach. Now it was time for us to leave.

Vanishing from the Great Dome and arriving at the beach, I was shocked at the sheer number of merfolk arriving at the beach. There must have been over a hundred. And surprisingly, they didn't stop at the border of the ocean. On reaching it, they dug their hands into the sand and began crawling out of the water, their long, heavy tails trailing behind them like snakes. I was amazed by the speed at which they were able to travel, almost as though they were amphibians. I didn't know how long they could survive out of water, and strangely—although many of them had started wheezing—they maintained their pace. It appeared that they were heading for the woods that lined the beach.

No. We can't have an infestation of these monsters. I'd seen how devilish these creatures were—my wife had firsthand experience during our quest to vanquish the black witches.

"Oh, God. Look!" Sofia clutched my arm and pointed further along the shore. I turned just in time to catch sight of a cluster of tails disappearing into the woods. All our witches were tied up with tackling the mermaids squirming along the sand in droves.

"They must not enter the island!" I bellowed. I lunged forward with Xavier and Sofia after the merfolk, who seemed to think that they'd escaped anyone's notice, even as I continued to rack my brain as to how these merfolk could have gotten here. First of all, why were they even in this area? How had they discovered The Shade, and how on earth had they managed to get inside the boundary?

I could only guess that somehow, the two merfolk already inhabiting our water had sent some kind of subaqueous signal and they'd come swarming in. And perhaps the pair Ibrahim had failed to catch were also the ones responsible for leading them in through the boundary.

Although the merfolk were fast, we were of course much faster, and they made a lot of noise as they scrambled through the undergrowth. We quickly caught up with them, grabbing hold of the ends of their tails—still slimy even after crawling across land.

They rolled onto their backs to face us, flashing their fangs and screeching. They lashed out, trying to maim us. My grip tightened around the tail of the merman I was tackling. Seeing that this guy wasn't going to play ball, I distanced myself from Sofia and Xavier and began hurling the merman round and round, picking up speed until he lifted off the ground. Then I knocked his head against a tree trunk.

That did the job. There was a dull thud as his head made

contact with the wood. He fell limp instantly. I could see that he wasn't badly injured—there was no blood spilling from his head. I'd only wanted to knock him out.

Xavier followed my lead, tackling his merman in a similar way, while Sofia fought with a mermaid. Both of them knocked the creatures' heads against trees, rendering them unconscious.

We lined up the merfolk together in a row before scanning the surrounding area to see if any had managed to escape our notice. Satisfied that these were the only ones who had managed to take this particular detour around our guard of witches and vampires, we picked up the stunned merfolk and carried them over our shoulders back to the beach.

Rows of captured merfolk covered the beach. Some were unconscious, some bound, while some appeared so still and injured I was certain they'd been killed.

"Did any others manage to enter the island?" My voice boomed across the beach.

"Don't think so!" came several shouts, between the screeches of the last of the merpeople putting up a fight.

Soon, all the merfolk were piled up together in the center of the beach. I cast my eyes out toward the ocean, unable to spot any more in the waves, although that certainly did not mean that there weren't more. It was more than likely that the merfolk we had lined up on the sand were only those who'd crawled out of the ocean before we arrived. Others could have just retreated into the depths.

"What do you suggest we do now?" Ibrahim called, brushing sweat away from his brow with the back of his hand.

I chewed on my lower lip, my eyes traveling over the long line of merfolk. From the looks of it, most had been stunned, but apparently in some cases where they had been caught by impatient vampires, they had been maimed and killed.

What now? I asked myself Ibrahim's question. *What are we going to do with all these fish?* The logical step would be to transport them outside the boundary, far away from our island, and drop them into the depths of the ocean. Then the problem of those merfolk who might still be lurking in our waters would remain. Ibrahim had already stated how difficult it was to catch them—and he'd only been talking about two merfolk. Here, we could be talking about a huge swarm of them. We didn't know. And it wasn't like we could send the dragons after them either, being protected by all this water...

"Not all of them lying here are dead," Xavier commented, "and we don't know how long it will take for those who were stunned to come to. We need to hurry and make a decision."

"We don't know how many more are still swimming within our boundary," Sofia said, looking anxiously out at the waves. "I think the first thing we need to do is set up a second boundary. A boundary that separates the water from the land. We need to prevent anyone from swimming at Sun Beach, or on any other shore of the island. I don't know what these merfolk are here for, or how they got inside, but it seems clear they want to enter the island. If we keep a second boundary up long enough, perhaps they'll go away..."

I had my doubts about that, and from the look on my wife's face, she did too. But she was right about what our first steps had to be. We had to secure the island immediately, which meant shutting off our access to the ocean.

Ever since The Shade was founded, we'd always had access to the stretches of water that surrounded the beaches. This would be the first time in history that we were forced to cut them off—for however long it took to get rid of this infestation.

I turned to Ibrahim. "You heard Sofia. The first thing we need to do is set up a second boundary. Not only must it prevent merfolk from entering the island, but it also must prevent any of our residents from entering the ocean. For now, we need to have a total lockdown. Other than the witches, the only persons with permission to exit should be Sofia, Xavier, and me."

Contact with the ocean was ingrained in our island's culture. Our people, especially the humans, enjoyed lounging around on Sun Beach and swimming in the waves. It would come as a shock to have that taken away from them without any warning, but it had to be done. I feared that even now, although it was evening, people might be swimming on some other part of the island and could be in danger of another attack.

"How soon can you work your magic?" I urged Ibrahim.

He exchanged glances with his fellow witches. "We'll get on it right away." With that, he and the other witches vanished, leaving the rest of us gathered around the line of merfolk and staring down at them grimly.

But we didn't have time to stand and stare. "We need to scour the beaches to check that the merfolk haven't simply migrated to another part of the island. In the meantime, ten vampires should stay here to make sure the merfolk don't escape. Once we've finished searching the island, and Ibrahim has confirmed that the second boundary is up, I'll return and give further instructions about what we're going to do with these creatures."

We formed a search party, while ten vampires volunteered to stay behind and keep watch on the merfolk on the beach.

Our search group split into two and began running in opposite directions. Each would work its way around the circumference of the island and we would meet again at the halfway point. Although I still hadn't turned back into a vampire and was technically a human, in addition to my ability to wield fire, my speed was nearly fast enough to keep up with a vampire— they lagged a little to keep up with my pace, but we were still able to cross the island quickly. I instructed everyone to keep a sharp ear and instantly report any screams or even the slightest sounds of struggle.

My throat was tight as we ran, my heart pounding. I kept expecting one of them to report an attack at any moment. Thankfully, we made it halfway around the island with no such alarm, and we didn't see any signs of an incident along the way. When we met up with the second party, led by Xavier, they hadn't come across any attack either.

Ibrahim came to us and informed us that the second boundary had been erected. Then it was time to deal with the merfolk we had left guarded by the other vampires. I arrived on the stretch of beach to find that most of the creatures had come to by now. Some had been bound, an attempt by the vampires to keep them in check. The latter all looked relieved to see me as I approached.

"So?" Ashley, who'd remained as one of the guards, asked, hands on her hips. "What are we going to do with these creeps?"

I was tempted to instruct the witches to hover the merfolk over the hunters' ships, still floating outside, and give them a nasty surprise. But of course, that was not the most tactful way of handling the situation.

In the end, I just had the witches transport them to the shore of a deserted island situated on the other side of the Pacific Ocean. I was certain that now that they knew where The Shade was, it wouldn't be too difficult to find their way back, especially if we had others still lurking within our boundaries who could call for them. But for now, this was the best we could do. In the meantime, we had to double down and try to figure out how to purge our water of any remaining merfolk. And until we did that, we were stuck with this hostile environment, feeling like prisoners on our own island.

Chapter 10: Rose

Caleb and I considered going to the meeting that my father had called in the Great Dome, but since they would only be discussing what we already knew, I didn't see any real reason for us to be there. I was aching for my brother as it was, and hearing the whole story repeated all over again would only end up making me more depressed.

So I suggested to my husband that we skip the meeting. Since our honeymoon, we had moved into our own treehouse. It was near my parents', and within the area of the Residences in general, but far enough away for us to feel like we were living alone.

I was still in the process of moving my stuff out of my old

room in my parents' penthouse. It was amazing how much I had accumulated over the years. I found objects under my bed that I'd forgotten I even possessed. The room was jammed with gifts from my eighteenth birthday combined with Caleb's and my wedding. My bedroom was large, but we'd received so many generous gifts, they had barely fit in my room. We had moved much of that to our new place already, but there still remained at least two loads' worth of stuff. I couldn't wait to hang up the painting of The Shade's Port that Anna and her family had created for me.

I could've asked one of the witches to help in moving the stuff, which would have been far quicker, but with everything that was going on in and around The Shade, I didn't want to bother any of them with such a trivial matter.

Seeing that Caleb and I had some downtime now, Caleb came with me to help move the rest.

"Do you actually need all this?" Caleb asked, scrunching his nose as he eyed the remaining possessions I had, some packed up in bags, some still strewn around the room.

I threw him a grin. "Why do you ask? We're not exactly lacking space in our new apartment. We've got to fill it up with something."

"Uh, no," he remarked. "There is a joy to space and simplicity. Not every room has to be cluttered like a trinket store."

I couldn't deny that I had already cluttered up our penthouse quite a lot, but I found it amusing that this was the first time Caleb was commenting on it.

He bent down and scooped up my hair straightener. He eyed it with a frown. "What's this?"

I moved up to him, taking the straightener from his hands and snapping it shut. "Oops," I murmured. "I didn't mean for you to see this. It's a kind of torture device wives keep for their husbands when they don't behave themselves."

He pulled me against him and pressed a kiss against the side of my neck. "You can torture me anytime," he said, his voice turning husky.

"Stop distracting me," I said, pushing him away even as I smiled from ear to ear. "I've been procrastinating on this job for weeks, I need to finally finish it off."

He gave me the eye before turning and surveying the rest of the room. "Well, we've already transferred most of it. I figure, what… twenty more trips and we should be done?"

I rolled my eyes. "Leaving aside all the gifts, I haven't got that much stuff, okay? At least not compared to other girls my age. You'd have a heart attack if you visited some of my girlfriends' bedrooms. We should be able to manage the rest in only two trips." I smirked as Caleb and I bent down to pick up armfuls of bags. "You know we sound like a legitimate married couple."

He smiled. "Maybe that's because we are one."

Caleb was, of course, grossly exaggerating the number of things I had. I was right in my estimation that we could carry the rest of the stuff in two more loads. This was definitely one upside to being a vampire: my strength. I was able to carry an inhuman number of things. And of course, Caleb, being larger, could carry much more.

We picked up as many things as we could and brought them back to our penthouse. We dumped them in the entrance hall before returning to my parents' apartment for the final load.

The final load.

Caleb began picking up bags and, strangely, I found myself stalling. Looking around my room, I realized that unless I went out of my way to come in here, this could easily be the last time that I set foot in this space.

It hit home for the first time that this was it—the final string that still attached me to my old, familiar life. In clearing out the last of my things, I truly would have moved on, into the next stage of my life. My life with Caleb.

Caleb eyed me, raising a brow. He set down the bags he'd picked up and approached me. He reached for my hair and tucked a strand behind my ear before sliding his hand down my jaw and tilting my chin up so I faced him. "What's wrong?" he asked.

"Nothing's... wrong," I said, my voice three tones deeper than usual. "It's just that..." I broke off. I didn't really know how to describe it. I wanted to move out, and I was over the moon to begin my new life with Caleb, but at the same time... it would be different. A permanent change to the only life I'd known. "What I'm feeling isn't bad or good, it's just... change."

From the look in Caleb's eyes, he understood. "I know what you're feeling," he said. "Change, however good, can be unsettling."

"Did you feel it too, like when you proposed to me?"

He shook his said. "Not when I proposed to you, or when I married you. I felt it when you initially suggested that I come live in The Shade. I don't need to remind you of how reluctant I was, even after realizing that the bond tying me to Annora's island had broken."

I nodded. At the time, he had given me a variety of excuses for his reluctance, like the bad terms that he and my father had left off on, and the general feeling that he just wouldn't fit in. I guessed at the end of the day, it had been a fear of change.

Caleb still had an expression of mild concern as he looked me over. He dipped down and caught my lips between his, kissing them gently as his hands traced my waist. He raised his head and gazed down at me through his warm, chocolate-brown eyes. He didn't say anything more, he just held my gaze, and my body close to him. And he couldn't have done anything better in that moment. The strength of his arms around me felt like an anchor, and the confidence in his eyes warmed me inside, causing the uneasiness in my chest to lift. I might have felt homesick to be leaving my parents, but Caleb's arms were the only home I needed.

I cleared my throat and returned his confident gaze. "I love you, Caleb," I said, draping my arms around his neck. "And nothing thrills me more than the thought of starting a life together."

I kissed him again. His arms tightened around me and he lifted me off the ground, kneading his lips passionately against mine. When he set me back down on my feet, he eyed the bags waiting for us and then my empty bed.

"What if you spent one last night here before we took the last of your stuff away?" he asked.

I bit down on my lower lip and looked over at my bed. It was slightly larger than a single bed, but it wasn't large enough to be considered double. I couldn't deny that the idea of sharing my last night in it with Caleb excited me. He hadn't spent much time in my room because we had been staying in one of the mountain cabins. I didn't know how long my parents would be gone. I took a guess that they'd sit in the Great Dome long into the night with the story they had to tell and the barrage of questions and discussion that would follow. I could just leave a "do not disturb" sign outside my bedroom door.

A coy smile curved my lips.

I looked deep into Caleb's eyes and nodded. "I'd like that. A lot."

We shifted the rest of the bags into one corner of the room, and since it was pushing late into the evening anyway, we took a long shower together and got ready for bed. Before we holed up in my bedroom, I took a piece of paper from the kitchen drawer and scribbled "do not disturb" onto it with bright red highlighter. I grabbed some tape and stuck it above my door knob before entering the room and closing the door behind me.

I smiled to see that Caleb had shifted the position of my bed. Rather than have it tucked away in one corner, he'd shifted it to the center of the room and placed a dozen lit candles around it. He must've rummaged around in the bags and found them. Although I'd accumulated a large collection of candles, mostly by way of gifts, the truth was I hardly ever got around to lighting them. I was glad that Caleb had taken it upon himself to find a good use for them.

I smiled even more to see Caleb already sitting on the mattress, leaning against the headboard. His bathrobe was slightly parted as it draped over his shoulders, revealing half of his muscled torso.

I doubted he knew how hot he looked leaning there casually, eyeing me steadily from across the room. If I'd been a human, I would've blushed a lot more as I crawled into bed.

I moved to lie on my side next to him, but he caught my arms and instead pulled me onto his lap, my back against his chest. He drew up his legs, allowing my lower back to slide down in between his thighs. His hands closed around my shoulders and glided down my arms before resting over my stomach.

I gazed around my bedroom. It looked so different with the bed shifted to its center and the candlelight dancing on the bare walls.

"So," Caleb began softly, his thumbs brushing against my lower abdomen through my silk nightie. "This is your last night in your room. What would you like to do?"

"Hmmm," I wondered, even as Caleb's touch made my skin tingle. "I suppose we could just… lie here and stare at the candlelight flickering against the walls all night," I suggested, trying to keep a deadpan expression.

"Certainly, we could do that," Caleb replied thoughtfully, his right hand moving slightly higher and resting over my ribcage, while his left continued to stroke my navel. "Or," he continued slowly. "We could perhaps… read a book together. Or play a card game. I noticed you have a few in the black bag."

"Hmm. I think playing a game is a good idea. But I don't think my card games are very good."

"Scrabble?" Caleb suggested innocently. "I spied that in the blue bag."

I twisted over onto my stomach so that I could face him.

"We could play truth or dare," I whispered, brushing my lips against his jawline. I drew away just before he could catch me and pull me in for a kiss. I eyed him teasingly as I pulled myself up higher over him. My legs on either side of his hips, I knelt on the mattress and rested my hands on his broad shoulders.

"Of course," Caleb replied, maintaining his innocent face, even as his hands roamed my haunches. "Ladies first, then. Truth or dare?"

"Dare," I replied.

"Very well," he said. "I dare you to… dance with me."

"Oh, come on," I said, trailing my hands down to his chest and flattening my palms against his bare skin. "That's not a good dare. I would dance with you anytime."

"All right," he said, his brows furrowing as though he were in deep concentration. "I dare you to…"

He was taking too long, and I was already growing impatient with this game. The way his hands roamed my body wasn't helping. I suspected that was his intention.

"All right, slow poke," I said, shifting on my knees against the mattress. "I will ask the question first. Truth or dare?"

"Truth," he said.

My eyes narrowed on him. I'd been hoping that he would choose dare. Now I was stuck playing a longer game.

"Okay. What was your first impression of me that night we met at the beach party in Hawaii?"

A smile crept over his lips, memory clouding his eyes. "You were drunk," he recalled, his smile broadening. "I could tell that you weren't used to drinking. When you came stumbling toward me over the sand and asked me to dance… half of me just wanted to tell you to go home." He broke out in a chuckle.

"That would have been mean!"

"You looked so out of place in that party. Barefoot, clumsy, disheveled hair glued against your sweaty face—"

"Excuse me!" I prodded his chest in mock admonition. "I didn't ask you to start insulting me."

"And yet," he continued, "I couldn't have found you more beautiful. Your innocence and unworldliness called to me, although I knew that I needed to stay away." His voice trailed off and his eyes took on a dreamy quality as he gazed at me.

I could have sworn that I felt a touch of warmth rising in my cheeks, but being a vampire, I must have been imagining it. I swallowed. "Okay. Now I'm going to ask you 'truth or dare' again, and you're going to choose dare, all right?"

He broke out in another laugh. "I don't think that's how this game is played, Rose."

"Well, Mr. Achilles, this is my slumber party, and this is how I want to play it… Truth or dare?"

His face became solemn. "Your ladyship requires that I answer dare."

Finally. I wasn't sure how much longer I could take his hands caressing my thighs.

I leaned in closer to his ear and whispered, "Make love to me."

I was glad that he didn't bother with any more banter. His hands slipped beneath my nightgown and parted it, baring me to him, while I stripped him of his robe.

I soon forgot that we were even still in my old bedroom. We could have been anywhere, back in our new treehouse, in the cabin of a boat—heck, even on the edge of a cliff. Caleb had such a way of consuming me that my brain seemed incapable of being aware of anything but the burning desire I held for him.

"Look how you're corrupting me, Rose," he breathed against my hair, as his tense body pressed against mine. "I thought we were here for a slumber party."

***

I wasn't sure how many hours passed before we finally rolled over onto our sides and drifted off to sleep.

But when I woke up, during what must have been the early hours of the morning, I knew immediately that something wasn't right.

The atmosphere felt thick and heavy, and as my eyes shot open, I realized that wisps of smoke were spilling into the room from beneath the crack in the doorway.

I clutched Caleb and shook him awake.

"We need to get out of here!" I urged.

His confusion turned to shock as he caught sight of the smoke filling the room. Leaping out of bed, he grabbed my hand and pulled me toward the door. He gripped the handle, pulling it ajar. Black smoke billowed inside. He closed the door immediately, even as I descended into a coughing fit. He placed his hand around the back of my neck and pushed me down toward the floor, where he crouched with me. Then he opened the door again. This time, through squinting eyes, I was able to see that the entire corridor was choked with smoke. And some feet away, coming from the direction of the living room, was the crackling of flames.

Oh, God. Where are my parents?

"Stay close to the floor," Caleb said. His grip around the back of my neck tightened and he pushed me closer against the floorboards. He crawled toward the bed and snatched up our nightclothes from the mattress. He draped my nightgown around me, slipping my arms through the sleeves, while he put on his own robe and fastened the pull string tightly around his waist.

"Try to breathe into the hem of your gown," he said. "Or better still, try not to breathe at all."

As a vampire, I could hold my breath for a long time. I couldn't have been more grateful for this ability as Caleb pushed open my bedroom door and we crawled out into the corridor. The smoke was so thick that it stung my eyes and made them water.

To our right, at the far end of the hallway, was a tall window, its Venetian blinds drawn. Caleb nodded in its direction, and we scrambled toward it. He made me stay on the floor while he reached up to pull open the blinds. But then he stalled. I gazed up to see what the matter was, and, to my horror, found myself staring through the glass at a wall of flames. The apartment was being consumed by fire from within and without.

Caleb grabbed my arm and pulled me back into my bedroom. We moved to the window in here. When we drew aside the heavy curtains, this window too was being licked by flames.

"What happened?" I breathed.

I didn't have the first clue as to what could have caused the fire. Fires were a very rare occurrence in The Shade. Even though we lived in trees, the witches had designed the penthouses to be fire-safe. I couldn't even remember the last fire that we'd had—other than when the dragons had stormed the island, though that hardly counted.

Fire inside the apartment, I could more easily wrap my head around. Perhaps there had been a gas explosion or something. But coming from the outside as well? What on earth had caused this inferno?

A coat of sweat broke out on my cold skin, and Caleb's forehead shimmered too.

"What do we do?" I gasped. "We're trapped."

If we took a left down the corridor and headed toward the exit of the apartment, we would meet with the fire within the penthouse, yet it seemed that we couldn't escape through the windows either without meeting with the blaze. We moved from room to room until we'd checked every single one on our side of the apartment, still untouched by fire, though becoming more and more choked with smoke each moment that passed. Each of the windows in these rooms looked out at the same flames.

I had been holding my breath as much as I could, but the fright and panic made it hard to regulate my breathing.

"We're going to have to brave the flames," Caleb said, his jaw set in a grimace.

The fire was encroaching both inside and outside the building, and we had to be quick. We checked the windows that we had access to once again, trying to find the window with the least amount of fire outside, but all looked just as deadly as the other. If we delayed any longer, we'd only make things worse for ourselves.

"Tie up your hair tightly," Caleb ordered as he tore the blanket from my bed. I didn't have a hair tie, but my hair was long and I managed to wrap it up in a tight bun. Spreading out the blanket, he began wrapping it around me, cocooning me in it. He grabbed three scarves from one of my open clothes bags and wrapped them around my legs and upper chest, securing the blanket against me, so securely that I was practically suffocating. He left enough of the blanket for me to pull over my head.

I gazed at him in alarm. All he wore was his thin robe. "What about you?"

Ignoring my question, he scooped me up and flung me over his shoulder. I felt useless, unable to move because of how tightly he was holding me. I couldn't see where he was going either with a blanket flapping in front of my face. But I sensed him hurry out of the room and back into the corridor. He moved along until he reached the window. The smoke had become so thick, I could barely see a foot in front of me.

Glass shattered, and then came a sharp spike in

temperature. I held my breath and shut my eyes tight.

"Cover your head!" Caleb hissed.

"Wait," I gasped. "What about you—"

It was too late. I only just managed to pull up the excess cover over my face and head before he leapt onto the window ledge and then took a dive off the building.

A wave of heat permeated my skin even through the thick blanket. I was terrified to think of the damage Caleb had just endured, and my chest ached for him as he let out a groan. We lurched into a freefall, Caleb's hold tightening around me, so tight that it felt like my ribcage would snap. My gut turned in somersaults until Caleb's feet hit solid ground with another painful jolt to my stomach.

He immediately lowered me to the ground and gripped my sides, freeing me from the flaming blanket. I staggered to my feet, away from the blanket, and gazed at Caleb in horror. Every part of his skin that was visible was raw and blistered, and his robe was flaming. I lunged for him and ripped away the burning robe, even as I tried to be careful not to touch his skin and cause him any more pain.

He now stood badly burned and completely naked in the woods. I was still in a state of shock, part of me unsure if I was just trapped in some kind of vivid nightmare. Caleb winced as he looked over the burns marring his skin.

My eyes lifted back up toward the treetops, toward my

parents' penthouse—but I couldn't even make out the building. The blaze surrounding it was too thick. Chunks of burning debris showered down from the treetops to the forest ground.

"Where are my parents?" I asked, my voice rising to a hysterical pitch. "What if they're still up there?"

"We need a witch." Caleb picked up his singed night robe and rolled it on the ground, putting out the last of the fire. He pulled it back on before reaching for my shaking hand. "To the Sanctuary." He hurtled toward the woods, dragging me along behind him. My knees were weak and shaking, but with adrenaline urging me forward, I ran like I'd never run before.

As we whipped through the trees, I began to yell for help. I hoped that a witch would hear us before we got to Corrine's home.

I practically cried with relief when the familiar silhouettes of my father and mother came into view along the forest path. My grandfather was walking alongside them. They must have stayed out late due to the meeting and hadn't yet returned to the apartment. *Thank God.*

Their faces lit up with alarm as Caleb and I reached them. They gaped at our disheveled, burnt appearance.

"Fire!" I panted. "There's a giant fire eating up your apartment!"

Caleb's hold on my hand loosened. "You stay and explain," he said as he began sprinting away. "I need to get a witch."

I looked desperately from my mother to my father. "I've no idea what happened, but Caleb and I decided to spend the night in my old room and when we woke up, the place was burning. We need to hurry before it spreads to the other trees!"

My father's face drained of all color as my mother's breath hitched. My grandfather grabbed my hand. "We should start evacuating the surrounding treehouses," he said.

As the four of us raced back toward the Residences, I ground my teeth the whole way, praying that Caleb would be swift. Thankfully, he was. By the time we arrived at the Residences he was already there with Corrine. He'd reached the Sanctuary and then traveled back here by magic in the time it took us to arrive.

Water shot from the witch's palms in torrents as she hovered in the air, aiming at the blaze. Although her efforts extinguished some of the fire, it was so monstrous, even her water wasn't enough.

She looked down at us on the ground. "I need to get help," she bellowed.

With that, she vanished, leaving us staring up at the wreck that had been my parents' beautiful penthouse.

Corrine seemed to have tamed the blaze enough for it to

not be an immediate danger to nearby trees, but Aiden hurried toward the neighboring treehouses to evacuate them all the same.

As I gazed up at the crumbling apartment, my eyes—still stinging—glazed over. I was sure that there wouldn't be a single thing salvageable from this wreckage. Everything my parents owned, all the furniture, all our books, all the important papers in my father's study, would be gone. Thankfully, Eli always kept backups of the most important papers relating to running the island in a safe in his own treehouse.

Corrine returned with Ibrahim, Shayla, and four other witches. Together, they doused the fire with torrents of water. By the time the flames were finally extinguished, it felt like an age had passed. A lone tear rolled down my cheek as I gazed up at what was left of the penthouse—of my childhood home. Practically nothing had survived. It had disintegrated into ashes, and even the tree trunk beneath the building had been scorched to a crisp.

My gaze traveled to my mother, who was looking too shaken for words. My father's face was stoic as he stepped forward, staring up at the wreckage.

"First the stolen chairs," he murmured, his voice low and somber. He cast his eyes toward my mother. "And now... this?"

My mother bit down hard on her lower lip. My father's expression turned from contemplation to anger.

Now that the fire was extinguished, I was desperate for one of the witches to treat Caleb. His natural healing capabilities had faded his burns somewhat, but he was still nowhere near healed. But before I could beckon one of them to come down from the tree tops to help him, an anguished howl pierced the night.

We all froze, eyes wide, and turned toward the source of the noise. It sounded like it was coming from the other side of the woods, from the direction of the mountains.

I'd never seen my grandfather look more terrified than in that moment. I wasn't yet able to recognize werewolves on the basis of their howls, but it seemed that my grandfather had developed the ability. His eyes bulged and he gasped, "Kailyn!"

Chapter 11: Rose

We jolted toward the howls, which seemed to only be growing louder and more desperate. Aiden took the lead—he didn't even wait for one of the witches to quicken our travel. We all followed him, except for my father, who stayed behind to beckon the witches down from the ruined penthouse, where they had been ensuring that not a single burning ember remained.

My father and the witches caught up with us. My mother grabbed hold of Aiden and slowed him down so that the witches could transport us to the mountains using their magic. We vanished and arrived a moment later in the clearing on the other side of the woods, at the foot of the

Black Heights.

"Oh, my God," I gasped. My eyes traveled up the mountainside and fell on another blaze. A fire had completely enveloped a mountain cabin. Aiden and Kailyn's.

"No," Aiden breathed. He bolted forward up the mountain while we hurried after him. When we arrived outside the cabin, the intensity of the fire scorched my skin once again. I caught Caleb's hand and pulled him farther back. His skin had suffered enough already.

The blood-curdling howls of Kailyn became strangled, and then halted.

"Kailyn!" Aiden yelled. He would've dove straight into the inferno before the witches had managed to extinguish it were it not for my parents holding him back.

The witches hurriedly emitted more water from their palms and poured it over the cabin.

Please let her be okay. Please let her be okay, I prayed in my mind. My grandfather couldn't take another heartbreak.

I glared at the fire, even as its heat dried out my eyeballs. I hadn't been able to observe the witches closely when they had put out the previous fire, because low-hanging branches had obscured many of the details of the scene. But here, out in the open, I was stunned by just how stubborn these flames were. Even as the witches flooded the cabin with torrents of water, more fire sprang up in its place. It wasn't like I had much, or even any, experience in putting out fires—although before turning into a vampire, I'd sure had the ability to start them—but these flames just didn't seem normal. They had wrecked my parents' penthouse so thoroughly, and they fought so steadfastly, even against the witches' magic.

And how did they even spark up in the first place?

I didn't understand what my father was talking about when he mentioned that his and my mother's chairs were missing, and I hadn't had time to ask, but I didn't need to be a genius to conclude that someone on this island was behind this. And as Corrine called to Ibrahim over the blaze, "There's magic behind these fires," my suspicions were confirmed.

Finally, they put out the fire enough for Aiden to race up the patio steps and kick open the door. We followed him in, gazing around at the devastation. Everything was scorched coal-black, and I could hardly spot a single recognizable piece of furniture. I couldn't imagine how anyone could survive this—vampire, werewolf, or heck, even a dragon shifter in his humanoid form.

"Kailyn!" Aiden boomed as he ripped through the cabin, barging through doors and turning over crumbling furniture.

The cabin was small and, with all of us inside, it took us less than a minute to search it in its entirety. I found Kailyn first. I spotted her beneath the bed in the second bedroom. In her wolf form, she was curled up in a ball. Her beautiful glossy, honey-brown fur had turned as black as the rest of this place. And she was still. Too still.

I tried to find my voice to call out to the others, but it caught in my throat. I stood up and grabbed hold of my mother, who stood nearest to me, by the arm. I pulled her down to the floor and pointed under the bed. She cursed beneath her breath—one of the rare times I'd ever heard my mother curse—and yelled for the witches.

Everyone flooded into the room, Aiden at the lead. He lurched toward the bed and attempted to duck down and look beneath it, but I threw myself against his chest and forced him backward. I couldn't bear for him to see Kailyn like that. I didn't know what it would do to him.

He gripped my shoulders and tried to push me away, but I held on tight, and my mother soon hurried over to assist me in restraining him. With the witches gathering around the bed, even as they hauled the wolf out from beneath it, Aiden's view was blocked.

"Let go of me!" he growled.

"We're taking her to the Sanctuary," Corrine said, even as her voice cracked.

"I need to see her!" Aiden demanded.

Corrine turned on him with anguished eyes. She swallowed hard. "Please, Aiden. Just give us some time to treat her. I promise you can see her after that."

***

After the witches vanished with Kailyn, my mother and I let go of Aiden. He bolted immediately for the exit and ran out of the cabin. Of course, he would head for the Sanctuary.

Tears blurred my vision as the rest of us hurried after him. I wasn't sure what the witches were planning to attempt, but I couldn't imagine how they'd be able to resuscitate her.

We whipped through the woods and arrived in the courtyard outside the Sanctuary. Aiden was already at the door, banging his fists against it.

"Open up!" he demanded in a shaking voice.

My mother and I tried to offer comfort, but he shook us aside. He just stood there, yelling for the witches and glaring at the locked door.

Corrine opened the door after five minutes, by which time Aiden was on the verge of breaking the door down. He barged past her and sprinted along the corridor. We followed him. My breathing was restricted, my palms sweaty as we neared Corrine's treatment room. Ibrahim stood outside the closed door, one hand on the handle. His face was ashen. As his eyes traveled slowly from Aiden to us, I already sensed that all hope was lost.

Swallowing hard, Ibrahim opened the door, allowing Aiden to burst inside. My grandfather froze at the foot of the treatment bed. As the rest of us piled in after him, we laid eyes on the large form of Kailyn, covered with a white sheet. Aiden staggered to the side of the bed. His hands shook as he reached for the corner of the sheet. He lifted it up slowly, and as he laid eyes on the werewolf, he stopped breathing. His body became rigid, as if a witch had just cast a spell of paralysis over him, and a deathly silence filled the room. It took some time for his shock to turn into grief, but when it did, he staggered backward, his legs hitting the edge of a chair, which he slumped down into.

I hurried over to him as he buried his head in his hands, his chest and back heaving with silent sobs. I couldn't hold back my own tears anymore. I draped my arms around his neck and kissed his cheek, holding him tight, while my mother did the same.

"I'm so sorry, Aiden," Corrine croaked. "I'd hoped there was a chance that we could resuscitate her, but… we were just too late."

Chapter 12: Ben

Despite the sheer size of the ogres, they were surprisingly adept at climbing down mountains. Their hands and feet were wide and tough, their skin so thick that it was almost like padding, allowing them to fearlessly gain a grip on even the sharpest rocks.

After I followed the beasts down the mountainside, it wasn't long before we arrived at the borders of a human settlement. A ski resort of some sort. We arrived in the midst of a blizzard, which worked to the ogres' advantage.

As soon as we reached buildings, they headed down an alleyway. I had no reason to follow them anymore. I scoured the small town, looking for a tourist shop of some sort. I found one next to a coffee shop in what appeared to be the town square. It was small and warmly lit, displaying all sorts of trinkets, but most importantly souvenir compasses, postcards, and maps. I was in Canada, not far away from Mount Logan, by the looks of it.

At least now I knew where I was. The next thing I had to do was figure out how to reach home. It was endlessly frustrating not being able to pick up any of the maps in the shop. Somehow, I was going to have to figure this out myself.

First, I had to make my way to the west coast of the country, but then once I arrived at the shores of the Pacific Ocean, I had no means of navigation. I could find The Shade in a submarine or almost any type of vessel, but without any navigation equipment? I had nothing now, just the knowledge that I needed to head westward.

Feeling overwhelmed, I reined myself in and forced myself to take things one step at a time. First reach the ocean, then figure out how to make it back to the island.

And so I headed west with as much speed as my subtle body was capable of. At some point, I had to reach the shore.

I did, in far less time than I could have anticipated. I arrived at a deserted beach, and, scanning the length of it, I knew that now I needed to find a harbor. I continued traveling and came across a large commercial port after an hour or so. I roamed around the ships, listening in to conversations and trying to figure out where each one was headed. I found one captain discussing his pending journey to Hawaii. Since this seemed to be the ship going nearest to The Shade, I stuck with him for the next few hours, until his break was finished and he returned to a massive cargo ship.

I moved on board and headed to the front of the ship, waiting for the journey to begin. To my annoyance, I waited another couple of hours. When the vessel did finally set off, its pace was horrifyingly slow. Slower than I'd ever imagined even a cargo ship traveled. I waited another couple of hours, and then, frustrated out of my mind, I found the control room and took a look at the maps and navigation equipment. I found myself again aggravated that I couldn't reach out and touch anything in my search for directions. All I could do was gain a general sense of direction from the display monitors—though it hardly helped even in the slightest. I already knew the general direction of Hawaii, and, consequently, the general direction of The Shade.

Although the idea of getting lost in the middle of the Pacific Ocean chilled me, even that was a more tempting proposition than staying here on this snail-slow ship. With my supernatural speed, I couldn't help but wonder whether, even with no means of navigation, traveling alone might be faster than remaining here. The vessel, in addition to being slow, wouldn't even take me to my final destination. It would take me to Hawaii, closer to home, but I would still need to figure out the final stretch by myself.

I gazed out toward the ocean, stalled. *Am I really mad enough to try this? This is the Pacific Ocean I'm talking about.*

I should've tried to reach an airport to get a ride on a plane to Hawaii. But I was already on the ocean now. I didn't want to spend more time searching for an airport on land—I had no idea where the nearest one would be, nor any immediate means of finding out.

Leaving the control room, I hovered upward into the air and looked down on the massive ship. Even if straying from the vessel did end up getting me lost, what was the worst that could happen? I was already a ghost. I no longer had the restraints of a physical body holding me back. The sun could not harm me. I didn't need blood, food, or water. I could survive… forever, I guessed. Even if it took me weeks to find The Shade, it wouldn't be the end of the world.

My mind made up, I drifted apart from the vessel, and as I sped up my sprint over the waves toward the endless blue, I looked over my shoulder and watched it fade into the distance.

I lifted myself higher up in the air. Since the sky was clear, I had a bird's eye view of the ocean and any surrounding land formations that might crop up.

Judging by the sun, I was racing southwest—or what I

hoped was southwest—the entire afternoon before something made me slow and freeze in midair. A sound. A tune? Drifting over the waves came a faint, enchanting melody. I tried to place what instrument it was. It sounded closest to a flute, though this guess was not quite right. The melody was soft and somber, distant yet haunting… breathtakingly beautiful. It spoke of life and promise, like the singing of a nightingale in spring. Even as I listened to it, it filled my heart with unexpected hope. Hope for what exactly, I didn't know, but the soulful tune so completely possessed my mind that I felt like I could hope for anything.

Where is it coming from?

I gazed around the water again, as if expecting to see a Pied Piper floating toward me on a fishing boat. From what I could see from my elevated position in the sky, there was no land for miles, nor any vessels on the waves. And yet the sweet melody continued. I wasn't sure if I was just imagining it, but it seemed to grow louder, penetrating the atmosphere and engulfing me, as though it was reaching inside me, touching my very soul, and filling me with an unexpected warmth.

It was coming from the direction I was headed. Southwest.

I continued on my journey. Spurred on by the exquisite tune, my speed reached levels that I hadn't even known that I was capable of. I wondered if anybody else could hear it, if they were present. Or was this just a product of my imagination? Was I just so desperate to reach home that I was imagining someone beckoning me back there? But, with the tune still in my ears, I wasn't capable of thinking much. I just wanted to listen, the cheerful notes lighting my mind up like a drug.

I couldn't have known how much time passed, but after what felt like an hour, the melody died as suddenly as it had started. Its absence sent my mood crashing down. The euphoria drained away, and I was left feeling hollow, alone in this world of dark, foaming waters. The sun had set by now. The moonlight trickled through my hands, making them appear paler and almost luminous in its reflection.

I felt more lonesome than I ever remembered feeling that night as I continued on my journey. But then, as dawn showed its first signs of breaking over the horizon, the melody returned. It called to me again, silently at first, then growing louder, until it grew to a pitch greater than ever before. Once again, the beautiful notes filled my mind and sent a rush of happiness flowing through me. Like an explosion of fireworks in my mind, the sound sent my mood soaring. I gazed out at the sun taking its place in the sky, and although I'd seen such a dawn arriving over the ocean many times before, I had never appreciated its beauty as much as I did that morning.

The melody grew louder still, until it was positively ringing in my ears, as though I was closer to it somehow.

I swept my eyes over the waves glistening in the early morning sun. And then I noticed it, far in the distance. A group of five grey ships. Large ships. Naval ships.

Excitement welled within me. *Could it be?* I feared that perhaps the hunters' ships had abandoned their watch outside our island and moved to a different location. But as I scanned the water, my gaze fell upon a familiar rock that served as one of the landmarks for The Shade's boundary.

I'm back. I'm back.

I could hardly believe it. I hurtled forward, racing over the frothing waves past the hunter ships, headed directly for where I knew our boundary was. As I came within what I estimated was twenty feet of it, a chilling doubt entered my mind. *What if I can't enter it? I was able to enter and leave before, having been granted permission by the witches, but without my human body, will the spell keep me out? Or perhaps boundaries don't work for subtle beings…*

Thankfully, my fear was unfounded. I passed through the boundary and found myself on the other side, enveloped in the darkness of The Shade. As I set my focus on the island's shore, the melody reached a feverish pitch, so loud that it had lost its soothing quality and become almost uncomfortable to hear. I found myself wishing that I could turn down the volume, or at least cover my ears, but of course, I could do neither.

As I arrived at the Port, the tune stopped once again. As before, it had only lasted a short while. Perhaps it would disappear for another day, or perhaps now that it had led me back, it wouldn't play again. Again I found myself wondering whether it was the strange work of some fragment of my own subconscious before I shook the thought aside and focused on whizzing through the woods. River and my family. I needed to find them.

I wasn't sure where River might be staying, but I guessed she'd be with the rest of the humans in the Vale—assuming she and her family had decided to stay in The Shade. Though, as a half-blood, I couldn't imagine River leaving anytime soon. She had to discover a cure first.

I passed by the Residences first and approached the foot of my parents' penthouse—my old home. Gazing upward, I almost yelled. Where the treehouse had been was the wreck of a fire. And scattered all around me in the undergrowth was scorched debris.

What on earth happened? Where are my parents? Where is Rose?

As I gazed around, all of the other treehouses seemed to have remained intact. Had this been an accident, my parents' penthouse going up in smoke? But what kind of accident could have caused this? In all my life, we'd never come close to even a single accident involving fire in our treehouse. And how long ago had the fire been? From the looks of it, this destruction had been only recent.

I set my eyes on my aunt and uncle's penthouse, wondering if they might be staying with them. Drifting through the front door, I searched all the rooms. The apartment was empty. Fear and confusion gripping me, I headed back to the ground. I knew that my grandfather was supposed to be staying in one of the mountain cabins with his girlfriend. That was the next logical place to visit.

But on arriving in the clearing at the foot of the Black Heights, once again, I was met with a sight of horror. Another home had been scorched, just like my parents' had. A cabin on the mountainside. I didn't know if this was my grandfather's cabin, since I hadn't had a chance to visit it during the brief period I'd returned to The Shade from The Oasis. But what was the cause of all these fires? I was about to begin moving up the mountain when voices sounded behind me.

I whirled around to see Ibrahim standing with… my father. Relief surged through me. I hurried toward them, calling out, "Dad," as if by my sheer willpower alone, he would somehow be able to hear me.

He continued speaking with Ibrahim, oblivious to my presence. I set my eyes on the warlock. He was a channeler of magic. Was there any way that he might sense my presence?

"Ibrahim!" I bellowed as loud as I could, even as I stood two feet away from him. I stretched out my arms and tried to grab him, but of course my fingers drifted right through his body. He, too, remained oblivious to my presence.

I fell silent and focused on their words.

"First thing after the funeral this morning," my father said, his voice deep and sober, "we will begin the investigation."

Panic arrested me again. *Funeral? What happened?*

My father's eyes rested on the wrecked cabin, a deep scowl marring his face. "Whoever is behind this will pay."

"What's going on?" I spoke aloud, even though I knew they couldn't hear me. "Where's Mom? Where is Rose? The rest of our family? River? Is everyone okay?"

There was a span of silence between the two of them as they both stared at the remains of the fire before they turned on their heels and headed back toward the woods. I followed them, hoping that they would lead me toward the rest of my family, where I could verify that they were all right. But then Ibrahim touched my father's shoulder and they both vanished, leaving the trail cold once again. Though not as cold as before. Perhaps Ibrahim had taken my father back to the Sanctuary? I figured that Corrine's place—particularly the courtyard outside—was usually used as the base for funerals. It made sense to head there.

I raced back through the woods and reached the courtyard

outside Ibrahim and Corrine's home. I stopped outside their front door and paused for a moment, attempting to steel myself for what I might find on the other side.

I glided through the door, emerging at the beginning of a long corridor. I heard the crying of an infant, but also that of a woman. I hurried along the hallway toward the source of the noise.

The baby's cries were coming from the fifth room on my right. Its door was ajar. I moved inside to find my aunt lying in bed and cradling in her arms a beautiful baby. *My new cousin.* He or she was wrapped in a blanket, and I couldn't make out the child's gender. I moved to the foot of the bed. Vivienne appeared tired and drained, though her eyes were brimming with affection as she cuddled up with her newborn. I wondered how long ago she had given birth. I gazed down at the child's face, and wished that I could have greeted my cousin.

Although I wanted to stay in the room longer, even if I couldn't hold the baby, the crying of the grown woman was eating at my nerves. I left my aunt and cousin alone and returned to the corridor. The sobs sounded like they were coming from Corrine's treatment room. My anxiety intensified as I approached it, trying to figure out if I recognized the voice.

I reached the end of the corridor and turned the corner to

find myself standing in front of my grandfather, sister, and mother. The three of them sat on a narrow bench against the wall. Aiden's head was resting in his palms, and his chest and back were shaking silently with… sobs? My sister and mother sat on either side of him, their arms wrapped around his midriff. I didn't understand the source of my grandfather's grief, but I felt relieved to have verified that all of my family was okay and had survived the strange fires—assuming that Xavier was somewhere around and in good health too.

I wanted to stop and just be with my sister, mother and grandfather, even if they couldn't see or hear me. But I had to keep moving. I had to find out what had happened here. I left them and moved into the treatment room, finally arriving at the source of the woman's crying.

Kira, the werewolf, was bent down over a large, teak coffin. Her cheek rested over the wood, her curly blonde hair spilling over the side of the casket. Her body shuddered with sobs. Micah knelt next to her on the floor, his arms around her, trying to offer her comfort.

"My sister wasn't ready to go," she rasped. "She had too much left to live for!"

Her sister.

It was Kailyn who died.

My gaze traveled to Corrine, who sat perched on the edge of the treatment bed. Her hands were clasped tightly in her lap, and her lips were pursed as she gazed with mournful eyes upon the grieving werewolf. I stayed for several moments longer before leaving the sorrowful scene.

Who would have killed Kailyn? Was this really not an accident? My father certainly didn't seem to think so.

As I arrived back in the corridor, it was to see my father again, standing next to Aiden, my mother and sister. He leaned against the wall, looking down with a pained look on his face at my grandfather, whose face was still covered by his palms.

We all knew how much heartbreak my grandfather had suffered in the past due to his first love, Camilla Claremont—my grandmother. After she'd died, he'd struggled for years—almost two decades—to let another woman into his life again. For him to lose Kailyn, whom he'd appeared to have truly fallen in love with, was a cruel twist.

I gazed down at my shattered grandfather. I wasn't sure how long it would take him to recover from this. Another two decades before he was willing to lay his heart on the line again for someone? What if he never recovered? He was a strong man, one of the strongest I knew, and he'd always been an inspiration for me, but behind his steely exterior was a broken man. When he'd met Kailyn and fallen for her, we'd all hoped that his heart was on its way to healing… but now I wondered if he would ever open up to anyone again.

I reached out a hand and moved it over his shoulder. I wished with all that I had that he could feel my touch—even just the smallest squeeze of reassurance, of empathy. My mother, father and sister, I wanted to hug them, too. I wanted them to see that I was alive, that I was home. I found myself starving to reconnect. To feel the ground beneath my feet. To stop feeling like I was a wisp of smoke, at risk of dissolving with the slightest gust of wind.

But hovering my hands over their arms and shoulders was the closest that I could come to contact without my translucent body sinking into theirs.

I stayed with them in the corridor, standing and suffering my frustration, until Corrine emerged from the treatment room and said in a husky voice, "People are starting to gather outside. We should begin the formalities."

My father nodded grimly and exchanged glances with my mother. She stood up, leaving my grandfather sitting with Rose, and they both headed into the room where Kailyn's coffin waited.

Glancing again at my sister and grandfather, I hovered a hand beside my sister's face, motioning to brush my fingers against her cheek, before stepping away and heading for the Sanctuary's exit. As I arrived back in the courtyard, a large crowd was gathering. Witches milled, conjuring up tables and black gazebos.

Now that I had learned the extent of the damage that had been done by those strange fires—or at least it seemed that I had, for I hadn't heard mention of other casualties—I left the courtyard, now desperate to find River. I headed straight for the Vale and began wandering through the streets, trying to figure out which house she could possibly be staying in. I didn't bother looking at houses that I knew were already occupied—which was most of them. I walked straight to the few houses that, at least to my knowledge, had been vacant. I arrived in the square, passed Anna and Kyle's house, and took a turn down a narrower street. About halfway down this road, sitting on the doorstep of a three-bedroom townhouse, was River's younger sister, Lalia.

She had a coloring book propped up on her lap, and next to her was a lantern, shining light through the darkness. Her round face was scrunched in concentration as she shaded in pictures with fat crayons. She had a glass of what looked like orange juice sitting near her bare feet, along with a half-finished bowl of cereal.

So they are still here. I felt relieved. Though I hadn't thought that it was likely River would have returned to New York while still a half-blood, there had been a small doubt at the back of my mind.

I moved past Lalia through the open doorway. The scraping of a chair came from the kitchen at the back of the house. I headed toward it and entered. Dafne and Jamil sat together at the dining table, quietly munching on breakfast.

I passed through the rest of the rooms on the ground level before moving upstairs. It was there, on the landing, that I heard her voice. River's voice. If I'd still had a body, goosebumps would have run along my skin. As it was, the sound of River filled me with emotion. I wanted to rush to her, pull her body flush against me, and press my lips to hers. While I couldn't do the latter no matter how much I wished for it, I hurried into the room her voice was emanating from.

There she was, sitting next to a bed where her mother lay wrapped in blankets. River's graceful form was covered with a bathrobe, tied at her waist. Her dark hair streamed down her shoulders and it was wet, as though she'd just stepped out of the shower. I moved closer, my eyes falling upon her mother. She didn't look well. Her face appeared more drained than I'd ever seen it, and her neck rested stiffly on the pillows.

The girl I loved brushed a palm over her mother's forehead and said, "Corrine said the pain should be gone after tomorrow. She said your spine will be healed. You need to take another dose of her potion now."

Her mother nodded. "Thanks, honey."

River stood up and moved to the bedside cabinet. She pulled out a tall, glass bottle filled with a murky brown liquid, and a spoon. Holding out the spoon level in front of her, she filled it to the brim with the potion before guiding it into her mother's mouth. Nadia swallowed, a grimace settling on her face as she downed it.

"Augh. I need water." Nadia reached for a glass half filled with water next to her bed and chugged it down in a few gulps. She took a deep breath. "I'm definitely feeling better than yesterday anyway," she muttered. "Whatever Corrine put in this disgusting medicine, it's certainly working."

There was a pause as River resumed her seat next to her mother. She drew aside her bathrobe to reveal a slip she wore underneath and began drying her hair with the robe.

"So, Mom," she said as she rubbed her scalp, "do you still not believe in mermaids?"

Nadia coughed out a dry laugh.

River bundled the robe over her head in a turban and stood up. She leaned over the bed and kissed her mother's cheek. "I'm going to get dressed."

River crossed the room and left through the door. I followed after her as she headed down the corridor. She took a left and entered a room next door to her mother's. I waited outside. It was bad enough being a ghost, I didn't need to turn into a creepy stalker as well and watch her undress.

I waited a few minutes, until I guessed that she would have had time to change out of her slip and put on some clothes. By the time I entered, she was wearing a light gray t-shirt that hugged her curves and a pair of sweatpants. She pulled out a hairdryer and sat in front of her dressing table. She paused and gazed at herself in the mirror. The dryer fell loose in her hands.

I moved closer to her from behind, staring at her reflection and wishing that mirrors could reflect my form. She breathed out a heavy sigh, her beautiful turquoise eyes traced with sadness. Instead of turning on the dryer, she planted it back in the drawer. Sliding her elbows over the dressing table, she leaned her head against her palms, her fingers reaching into her hair and gripping it, her hands curling into fists. I bent down lower, trying to take in her expression. Her eyes were scrunched up tight, her lips pressed together and trembling slightly, as if she was trying to hold back a sob.

"River," I breathed. I laid my wispy hand on her shoulder, wishing more than ever that my fingers could close around her in even the gentlest touch.

She drew in a deep, harried breath and raised her head, once again facing the mirror. Her eyes had become full with tears, and one spilled slowly down her cheek.

She brushed it away with the back of her hand and stood up, moving to the window. Resting her palms on the windowsill, she stared through the glass over the surrounding rooftops of the Vale and toward the towering wall of treetops beyond.

I stood behind her, my chest grazing her back. I ran my hands down along her arms and lowered my mouth against the back of her neck. She shivered suddenly and took a step back—passing right through my body. She moved to the single bed in the corner of the room and pulled off a blanket, which she draped around her shoulders.

Did she feel my presence just now? Does my form emit a kind of coldness? Or was it mere coincidence? Being a half-blood, she was almost always cold, after all.

When she moved away from the bed, she didn't return to the window. She stood in the center of the bedroom and gazed around, as though she didn't know what to do with herself.

I remained by the window, just gazing at her. After I had made River leave The Oasis with Corrine and I'd taken off on my crazy journey into the supernatural dimension, I'd honestly believed that I would never see this girl again. And while I couldn't have imagined in my wildest dreams reuniting with her in these circumstances, I felt grateful to be standing in front of her. Even if I couldn't reach out and touch her, kiss her, hold her in my arms and tell her how much I ached for and loved her, just being able to lay eyes on her again and see that she was safe was more than I'd hoped for.

She slumped to her knees on the floor, staring blankly at

the opposite wall. As another tear escaped down her pale cheek, her lips parted slightly and I could have sworn that she breathed my name. I could only assume that her tears were for me.

Chapter 13: Ben

I stayed with River in her bedroom until she finally picked herself up off the floor and walked back to her mother's room. As much as I ached to stay with her, now that I had seen that those I loved most on this island were safe, I had to start figuring out some answers. *What is really going on here*?

It seemed that the funeral had been very last-minute, and many of the humans were going about their day as though nothing had happened. Perhaps word of Kailyn's death hadn't yet spread past the supernatural community. Or perhaps my parents were deliberately holding back the news until after the investigation my father had spoken of with Ibrahim, so as to not plant unnecessary worry or fear in the minds of our human population.

I hurried back through the forest and arrived in the courtyard outside Corrine and Ibrahim's home where the funeral ceremony was in full flow. Kailyn's coffin had been placed in the center. I caught sight of Aiden at the front of the crowd. His eyes were red, but the rest of his face was quite expressionless. Stony, cold.

A few feet away stood Kira, who was still sobbing into Micah's arms. He stroked the back of her head as he held her tight.

My parents also stood in the front row, along with a teary-eyed Rose and a grim-looking Caleb—whom I was seeing for the first time since arriving back.

Among the sea of other familiar faces, I also caught sight of Abigail Hudson. This was the first time I'd seen her since the day I'd first left The Shade all that time ago. She was standing a few rows back from the front, next to Erik. He had an arm around her waist while she rested her head against his shoulder. Both of their gazes were on the ceremony, their expressions worried and somber. I was pleased to have the chance to see her again. While the romance between us had never worked out, Abby and I had become good friends before I'd left. I'd wondered how she had been doing, and to see her in the arms of Erik was comforting. I was glad that she had found someone else, and if Erik was anything like the man Kiev had turned into for Mona, I was sure that he would make her happy.

Drawing my eyes away from Abby, I was about to move closer to the center of the courtyard through the crowds when my hearing was assaulted with a deafening tune. The same tune that had beckoned me across the Pacific. It started up again, louder than ever before. As was the case the last time I heard this melody on arrival within the island's boundary, it was no longer beautiful to me. It was far too loud for me to appreciate it. It rang in my head so intrusively, I barely had room in my mind for my own thoughts.

Where is that sound coming from?

I glanced around the funeral ceremony once more and figured that now was as good a time as any to find out. I moved away from the courtyard, turning in a circle and straining my hearing to ascertain which direction the noise was coming from. It definitely wasn't coming from anywhere near the beach behind me. No. The melody was coming from the mainland, its shrill tones piercing through the trees behind the witch's temple. I followed the sound as best as I could, through miles of dark woods, until I neared the part of the island that was designated for agriculture. The trees thinned and gave way to meadows of corn and wheat, sprawling orchards, and a sea of vegetable fields. It was by the witches' magic that we were able to grow such fresh produce without the rays of the sun.

I paused, trying to find my bearings. The tune was drifting toward me from the direction of the vegetable fields. I moved forward swiftly again, my feet grazing the soil. I passed through several fields, until the melody reached a fever pitch and stopped. My mind stopped ringing and the quiet, soothing sounds of the island returned.

But it meant that I'd lost the trail again. Now I might need to wait hours before it started up... although it had sounded so close to me. It'd been louder than ever a few seconds ago. I was certain that it came from somewhere in these very fields surrounding me.

I stopped amidst the potato crops and scanned the area once again. To my left was a thin line of trees, marking the border between the potato and cauliflower fields. At the end of this row of trees was a small farmhouse that hadn't been inhabited for decades. Although I'd spent most of my life on this island, I was quite sure that I had never stepped inside of it, even as a child.

Then I spotted something strange. Gathered beyond the building, deeper into the cauliflower crops, was a crowd of people. Except, as I moved closer, they weren't exactly people. They were... ghosts. Perhaps fifty of them, all hovering near the farmhouse.

I was momentarily stunned. I found myself rooted to the

spot, just staring at this odd crowd. There were men and women of all ages, and even some children. Some wore casual, modern clothes like jeans and t-shirts, while others wore outfits that looked like they belonged in the eighteenth century; the women wore long, heavy frocks, while men donned breeches, cravats, and pleated coats. The only thing in common was that their attire looked ripped and ragged, and sometimes even stained with blood. That, and they all appeared to be humans, or rather had been humans in their former lives.

What in the world…?

Through my confusion, I realized that this was the first time I'd thought about the fact that ghosts even wore clothes. I looked over my own form. I was wearing the same clothes I'd worn before leaving my body—a cloak, ripped shirt and pants—only now the fabric had almost become a part of me. The garments were just as intangible and wispy as the rest of my form. I couldn't take the clothes off, or even touch them—my hands just ran through them, as they did with everything else I tried to make contact with. It appeared that ghosts took on an identical appearance to the body they left behind. Almost like some kind of distant reflection, a shadow of their former selves.

Heads turned toward me as I arrived within ten feet of the crowd. They looked me over curiously.

"Who are you?" I asked in a hushed tone—hushed not because I had any reason to be quiet, but because I was still in a state of surprise.

I received several frowns before spirits from the crowd began calling out their names. "Augustus Croft. Tiffany Adkins. Tim Forney. Charlie McGuire. Lucinda—"

I held up a hand. I really wasn't interested in knowing their names. "Wait, wait. I mean, where do you come from? Why are you here?" My confusion deepened as I gazed around at their bedraggled forms. "Did you all take the potion too?"

They appeared to be bewildered by my last question.

"Potion? What're you talking about?" The woman who'd called herself Lucinda stepped forward. She appeared to be in her late twenties, with ebony skin and curly black hair tied up in a bun over the top of her head. From her rich accent, I guessed that she was from the Caribbean. She wore a suit that reminded me of those worn by air stewardesses—a gray skirt and jacket with a brooch attached, and a blouse whose front was drenched in blood.

I tore my eyes away from the crimson stains. "Did you not take a potion?" I asked. "A light blue liquid administered by a witch. It separates a person from their body and turns them into a ghost."

She looked at me as though I was crazy. "I've no idea what

you're talking about," she said.

How could these people have become ghosts and not heard of the potion? From what Arron had told me, I'd gotten the impression that people who died normal deaths didn't become ghosts. That was what the potion was designed for—detaching a person from their body, but still allowing them to remain in their previous existence without moving on to… whatever awaited after death.

I glanced around at the other ghosts again. They also looked blank at my mention of the potion. Maybe there was another way to become a ghost after all. Maybe Arron had not given me the full picture. Perhaps he had not even known it himself.

"Where have you all come from?" I asked, trying a different tack.

Lucinda was the first to reply. "From 1982. I died in a plane wreck."

I raised a brow.

"The plane I was working on, chartered for Hawaii, crashed over the Pacific before we ever made it there," she explained.

"And that's how you became a ghost?"

Now it was the woman's turn to quirk a brow. "Uh, yes."

"But how?" I asked, more to myself than to her.

She shrugged. "How do I know? One minute I was being

thrown about the plane and the next, the pain vanished and I became… this." She eyed herself over.

I fixed my focus again on the other ghosts—particularly the section that did not appear to be from this century, or even the last.

"You didn't all die in the same crash. Where are the rest of you from?"

Lucinda gestured toward a group of eight ghosts behind her—two children, five women, and one man. "They were on the plane with me. Passengers. As for the rest of these people, I'd never laid eyes on them in my life until arriving here on this island."

An elderly man with an eyepatch over his right eye drifted toward me. He wore a beaver hat, a long-sleeved shirt, and black pants that stopped at his knees, beneath which were long brown stockings. "I died in a shipwreck, about two hundred years ago now. On a voyage from Japan to the Philippines."

"I suspect you'll find that most of these people here are from around the Pacific," Lucinda murmured.

I was still trying to wrap my mind around how they could be ghosts—but one thing that was becoming amply clear was that they all appeared to have died in some kind of traumatic, sudden way. Perhaps being ripped from the world unexpectedly caused one to become a ghost? I could only speculate because these ghosts didn't seem to have a clue as to the meaning behind their existence.

"And why are you all here on this island?"

"I suspect for the same reason that you are here," the old one-eyed man said as he glanced over me from head to foot. "Did you not hear that heavenly tune? Is that not what beckoned you to this strange, dark island?"

"I was wandering somewhere near the coast of Hawaii," Lucinda offered, her eyes growing distant with memory. "Not all that far from the plane wreck. Like the rest of us, I heard the melody calling to me across the waves. The most beautiful sound that I'd ever heard. I barely had a choice but to search for it. It was… like an angel calling me. I thought perhaps one had descended to finally end this half-life and coax me to heaven. I followed the tune for days. It disappeared sometimes and left me stranded in the middle of the ocean, but then it would start up again some hours later. Finally, I found this place. It is not heaven, but… it is somewhere I am meant to be. I cannot explain why, but as loud and shrill as the melody became on arrival… I do not want to be parted from it. I can't bring myself to leave."

"Where's the tune coming from?" I demanded. "Who is playing it?"

"The man with the pipe," one of the children of the air crash, to my right, squeaked.

My eyes shot toward her. "Man? Where?"

She raised a small hand and pointed toward the farmhouse.

The farmhouse. Leaving the crowd, I moved toward its front door. As I arrived outside of it, I caught the scraping of chairs against the floor. And then whispers that I couldn't quite make out. I drifted through the old wooden door, and, appearing on the other side, the first thing that met my eyes was a long woodwind instrument propped up against the peeling wall near the door. Its body was thick and perhaps three feet in length. It was made of polished black wood, and it reminded me of a bassoon.

My gaze moved deeper into the farmhouse's dank entrance room. The door to the living area was open, and from it glowed flickering candlelight. When I glided to the door and entered the sitting room, nothing could have prepared me for what I saw.

Jeramiah and the witch, Amaya, stood around two high wooden chairs.

Amaya wore a trailing maroon dress that covered her legs and arms and formed a turtleneck around her throat. Jeramiah was draped in a heavy black robe. The chairs they were gazing down at looked familiar. I could have sworn that they belonged to my mother and father—chairs they sat on during meetings in the Great Dome.

How did the two of them ever penetrate the boundary?

And what on earth are they doing here?

Chapter 14: Ben

I gaped at the couple as Jeramiah gripped the arm of one of the chairs. He turned it on its side and laid it down over the creaking floorboards.

"We will carve these now," he said to Amaya in a low voice.

"How much should I carve?" the witch asked.

"Of course, we won't need all of this wood. We'll take what we need and then burn the rest. Just be sure to cut shavings from both of them."

He left Amaya with the chairs and walked halfway across the room, where a round stone slab was propped up against the wall. He gripped its edges and laid it down gently on the floor before kneeling down over it and running his palms over its smooth, sanded surface. He glanced back over his shoulder at Amaya, who had already bent down with a sharp knife and was beginning to carve off shavings from the chairs. She worked quickly and with ease, as though she were slicing cheese rather than solid wood. Clearly she had placed some sort of charm over the knife. Within thirty seconds, she'd created a pile of splinters from both my mother's and father's chairs. She gathered them up in her palms and handed them to Jeramiah. He set them down on the floor, next to the round slab of stone.

"Hand me the adhesive," he muttered. "And also the sealant."

The witch picked up two cups that had been sitting on the dusty mantelpiece. One was filled with a thick white substance, while pooled in the other was a transparent, runny liquid.

"You'll also need a brush," the witch said as she placed the cups down next to the vampire.

She walked to one corner of the room where an old broom leaned against the wall. She turned it upside down, gathering strands of its bristles between her fingers, before yanking hard and detaching them from the wood. Reaching for her knife again, she cut off a long, thick slice of wood from one of the chairs, the tip of which she dipped into the bristles.

Magically, the bristles clung to the stick. She approached Jeramiah, holding out her makeshift brush for him to take.

Jeramiah dipped the brush into the thick, white liquid and ran it in strokes around the center of the stone. Then, collecting some of the shavings between his fingers, he began to lay them out on the sticky stone surface, slowly and carefully, in the forms of letters. The white adhesive dried quickly, becoming transparent, and soon I found myself staring down at the words:

In honor and memory of Lucas Dominic Novak.

Jeramiah reached for the sealant and brushed a generous coating over the wooden letters. Then he stood up and gazed down at the stone with brows furrowed and a thoughtful expression on his face.

"Add a few flourishes around the edges, will you?" he asked the witch after a pause. "Even with the letters, it still looks rather bare."

Amaya heaved a sigh and bent down over the slab, holding the same knife that she had used to cut my parents' chairs. She angled the blade against the stone, and again, as though the slab was made of butter, she began etching a pattern of ivy leaves around the edges.

"Good," Jeramiah breathed after she'd finished. His sharp blue eyes glistened slightly, and there was an odd warmth to them—warmth that I hadn't witnessed in my cousin before.

A span of silence fell about the room as Jeramiah continued to admire the slab, now turned into a memorial stone. Still gazing at the two of them in disbelief, I found myself holding my breath—as though I even had any to hold—like I was afraid they might hear me. It was Amaya who finally disturbed the quiet.

"Do you think that one last call will be enough?" she asked.

Jeramiah took in a breath, his eyes darting toward the wind instrument that rested near the front door. "It will have to be enough," he replied. "Nuriya's favor only stretches so far."

Amaya's expression was doubtful. "And what if it doesn't happen?"

Agitation played across Jeramiah's face. He shot a sharp glare at the witch. "Don't consider it."

He dipped down to the stone again and trailed his fingers over its now uneven surface. "It's perfectly dry now. It's time we head for the Great Dome. The ceremony is still going on, and we ought to do this before the funeral is finished."

"Wait," Amaya said, alarmed. "Now? During the day? I thought the plan was to do it at night. What if somebody enters the Dome?"

"You'll have cast an invisibility spell over the two of us. Worst comes to worst, someone enters the chamber and is unable to see us, but notices the stone. But I doubt it will come to that—not if we're done before the funeral ends."

Amaya still looked worried, but she didn't argue. She swallowed and sealed her lips.

Jeramiah headed out of the living room and crossed the hallway. He stopped at the woodwind instrument and, picking it up, stowed it in his belt, beneath his robe. Then he returned to the living room. He placed his hands either side of the memorial stone and stood up with it.

"Cast the spell now," he ordered Amaya.

As the witch's palms twitched, I was certain that she had cast the spell—yet I could still see both of them as clear as day. Apparently the vision of ghosts was not susceptible to being impaired by invisibility spells.

"Now vanish us to the Dome," Jeramiah said.

Amaya planted a hand on Jeramiah's shoulder, and both of them disappeared from the spot.

If I'd had a heart, it would've been hammering in my chest by now, blood pounding in my ears.

I need to reach the Dome.

I hurtled toward the nearest wall of the living room, and, passing through it, I emerged from the dilapidated farmhouse, reappearing in the dark field outside. The crowd of ghosts was still gathered round the building. They looked like they had hardly budged an inch since I had left them. Some looked after me as I whizzed across the fields, shooting toward the direction of the woods, while others even called out to me, but I ignored them all. I had tunnel vision as I urged myself faster and faster.

It was only a matter of minutes before I arrived at the Great Dome—but these were minutes when Jeramiah and Amaya could have been doing God knew what. When I entered the meeting chamber, it was empty, except for Jeramiah and Amaya standing right at the front, near the raised platform where my parents' chairs had been. In their place now rested the memorial stone Jeramiah had created for his father.

Two clusters of incense had been lit on either side of the slab—the thin sticks had been stuck into the cracks in the floor to keep them upright. Jeramiah, standing a few feet back from the memorial slab, his eyes calm and steady, appeared to be waiting for something. He was watching the two incense clusters intently, and it was only now that I looked at them more closely that I realized how quickly they were burning and how much smoke they were emitting. Clearly, these were no ordinary incense sticks. They were burning at the speed of a match, and as the sticks disintegrated, the room was choked with a thick smoke. I could only guess the kind of aroma that emanated from them, but as Amaya strangled a cough, I imagined that it would be overbearing. The smoke was so thick that I had to move closer to the couple to see what they were doing.

Jeramiah reached inside his robe and drew out the wind instrument. Raising the mouthpiece to his lips, he blew into it, and it sounded out louder than ever. So loud that I staggered back. This was the loudest I'd ever heard the melody, and certainly the closest that I'd been to it. I stared at the vampire as he played, his fingers moving skillfully over the keys, as if he'd played the instrument his whole life. From far away, the sound was breathtaking—more beautiful a tune than I could ever play.

According to the clock hanging from the wall, he played for only five minutes before he replaced the instrument within the folds of his robe. Silence overtook the Dome.

It was more than clear to me by now that this instrument was like a kind of dog whistle for ghosts. Nobody else could hear it—not even Jeramiah.

"Do you really trust that old yogi?" the witch asked.

Jeramiah's jaw twitched. He grunted curtly. "Throughout all the years I spent in India, he was the only true medium I came across. He knows more about ghosts than almost any supernatural. Yes, I trust him."

Doubt still flickered in the witch's eyes. "It's just that... I mean, you've been playing that thing every few hours for the last two days. How do you even know it's called anyone?"

"That will soon be clear to me," Jeramiah replied, his eyes

settled on the memorial slab. "Now we must be silent."

He lowered to his knees and tilted his head slightly downward before whispering words that sent chills down my spine. "Father, if you heard my call, make yourself known to me."

He's trying to summon... Lucas Novak?

Could it possibly be that my uncle became a ghost?

"Send me into a deep, dreamful slumber," Jeramiah said, his voice slightly raised as he addressed the witch. "I need to make myself available."

"What if somebody comes?"

"You're a bag of nerves, Amaya," Jeramiah said impatiently. "Just do as I say. We're invisible, for a start, but if somebody comes, even in my sleep you can transport me elsewhere to safety. But I don't wish to be unconscious for long. Watch the clock and wake me up in ten minutes. That will be enough time for me to know whether or not my attempts have been successful."

Amaya gulped, then nodded. Jeramiah lay on his back, stretched out directly in front of the raised platform where Lucas's memorial stone reigned over the room.

The witch fumbled her way over to Jeramiah and, feeling his form, placed both of her hands on either side of Jeramiah's head. Flattening her palms, she moved her thumbs up and down Jeramiah's forehead, slowly and gently, until it was clear that the vampire had fallen asleep. His breathing pattern changed, becoming slower, deeper, and the muscles in his face relaxed.

The minutes that followed were tense. Silence engulfed the room once again, leaving me to brood over what exactly Jeramiah was trying to accomplish by attempting to connect with his father's ghost. *And how did my cousin even get into The Shade to begin with?* I moved closer to him, daring to stand just two feet away and stare down at his face, still slack and expressionless. The smoke in the room was beginning to thin now, and I could see all the way across the Dome to the other side, where the entrance was. I half expected to see the ghostly form of my uncle strolling through it, but as the minutes passed, I saw no such thing.

Ten minutes went by, at which point Amaya approached Jeramiah. She reached down and touched his forehead, making the same gentle motion with her thumbs against his skin. His eyes shot open, and he sat bolt upright.

I could tell from the dark look that took over his face that he hadn't gotten what he wanted, and from Amaya's expression, she had realized that too.

"Well?" she whispered.

Jeramiah shook his head slowly. "Nothing." His voice was thick with disappointment.

"So what does it mean?"

Anger flashed in the vampire's eyes. "It means that when my father died, despite the sudden circumstances, he did not become a spirit."

Amaya frowned deeply. "I don't understand how you can just draw that conclusion," she said. "Any number of things could have gone wrong. To start with, what if his spirit simply wasn't close enough to hear your call? What if—"

Jeramiah shook his head, causing Amaya to trail off. "No. If my father became a ghost, he would've been hovering near The Shade. When people become ghosts, they feel bound to return to where they most consider home. Even despite the hostile environment that my father had to endure while living here, this was his home, and the only place in the world where his soul could have found refuge. I learnt enough from my teacher to know this to be a fact. Even if my father took a break from the island, he wouldn't have ventured far, and the call I made was powerful enough to have reverberated across the Pacific Ocean. He would not have missed it."

Amaya paused, crossing her arms over her chest. She ran her tongue along her lower lip, as though weighing her next words.

"So what now?" She cocked her head to one side. "I think you've caused enough destruction to this place... You've replicated the sense of hostility that your father endured, both surrounding and within the island—first by using my potion to attract swarms of savage mermaids, and then burning the homes of the islands' leaders to the ground. You also dishonored them further by destroying their thrones and using the wood to craft a memorial in honor of your father… Jeramiah." Her voice and gaze softened. "You have done enough for your father. Wherever he might be, I'm sure that he would feel avenged. Let's leave this place and allow his and your souls to rest in peace…" Amaya drew in closer and, feeling for Jeramiah's arm, aimed a kiss against his jawline.

Jeramiah's face was stony as ever, and he appeared unmoved. He remained rooted to the spot.

"Besides," Amaya continued, "as you already reminded me yourself, Nuriya's leniency only stretches so far. We have already extended our stay past the time you requested from her, and if you force her hand, I fear you'll regret it." She peeled back the end of her right sleeve and began rolling it up her arm. "I'm surprised our marks haven't been burning unbearably already…I'm just going to remove my invisibility for a second." After apparently removing the spell, she pushed the sleeve up high enough to reveal her right bicep. Gazing down at it, she gasped. I moved nearer to see what had surprised her, but I should have guessed… she no longer had a tattoo.

Shock registered in Jeramiah's eyes as he rushed over to the witch and gripped her arm, staring down at her bare skin. It was completely devoid of even the slightest trace of the black cross, as though it had never been there to begin with.

"Oh, my," the witch breathed.

Jeramiah let go of her, and, parting his robe, rolled up the sleeve of his shirt to examine his own arm. His, too, was devoid of any signs of the imposing tattoo that had once marred it.

He fell silent, his demeanor infused with thoughtfulness.

"Interesting," he said, his voice low. "Very interesting."

The witch still appeared to be in a state of shock and disbelief. "What could have happened?" she breathed.

"I can't be sure," he replied in a voice as quiet as hers. "But it doesn't matter. We are no longer bound to them. We are free."

"But—"

Amaya's response was cut short as the front door of the Great Dome rattled. Jeramiah swooped toward the memorial slab and the instrument so fast he was a blur. The next thing I knew, he and the witch had vanished.

Still in a daze of confusion myself, I turned to face the door to see my father striding in. He was followed closely by my mother, Xavier, and Vivienne, who was carrying her new baby wrapped in a blanket. Then entered Eli, Yuri, a heavily pregnant Claudia, Kiev, Mona, and dozens of other familiar faces. The only notably absent member of my father's council was my grandfather. Each of their expressions was leaden and somber.

By now, the smoke had completely cleared from the room, and if it had left behind any scent, none of them seemed to notice it. Nobody made the slightest comment as they all took seats around the long meeting table.

I would've stayed to listen to what they'd all gathered to discuss, but my mind was tied to Jeramiah and his witch companion. I had to know what they were going to do next. I guessed that there was only one place that Amaya would've vanished Jeramiah back to—the old farmhouse.

I hurried out of the Dome. Passing through its solid walls, I raced back into the thick of the woods. I didn't let up my speed until I had arrived back at Jeramiah's hideout. I didn't even bother to glance at the crowd of ghosts who were still waiting expectantly around the building. Passing through the old wooden door of the house, I found both he and the witch were in the living room again. Jeramiah was prowling the room like a panther, while Amaya was slumped in a chair, still appearing lost in a daze of relief and confusion. The memorial stone had been replaced in its former position, leaning against the wall.

"Something obviously happened to the jinn back in The Oasis," she murmured, "but can we really be certain that just because the tattoo is gone, our connection to them has also been severed?"

Jeramiah didn't stop pacing as he replied. "The absence of our tattoos doesn't necessarily equate to the absence of their hold on us... but why would the marks vanish so suddenly? Think about it, Amaya. What possible reason could the jinn have for revoking them? There is no reason." He shook his head emphatically. "No. I suspect that something serious has happened... Something that has weakened them, and caused them to recall their powers over others in order to reserve them for self-defense."

"But what could have happened?" the witch asked. "Do you think the Drizans found them?"

Jeramiah shot her a curious glare. "How do you know about the Drizans?"

"Oh, I've had an inkling about the Nasiris' adversaries for a few years now," Amaya replied. "I overheard a conversation that I shouldn't have between that little squirt of a niece Nuriya has and her mother."

"Interesting," Jeramiah said, momentarily distracted. "That loose-lipped jinni was the way I found out about them too...." He cleared his throat. "Anyway, if I have any theory at all, it's as you've described. I'm not sure who else would pose a threat to the Nasiris other than the Drizans. Yes, it is only a theory, but even if I'm wrong, I think we ought to take any risk that could come with staying away... I mean, would you really willingly venture back into their lair to verify our assumption?"

She shook her head. "Of course not."

Jeramiah nodded curtly. "Then, given the circumstances, I would like to propose that our stay on this island be… a little prolonged."

Chapter 15: Ben

Jeramiah once again drew out the wind instrument from beneath his robe. Holding it, he raised it in the air and in one abrupt motion, brought it crashing down against his knee. The wood cracked and the instrument broke into two. He discarded both pieces unceremoniously, dropping them to the floor and kicking them to the wall.

"Why did you do that?" Amaya asked, furrowing her brows in disdain.

"My father is gone," he replied, his voice baritone. "I have no further use for it."

The vampire's face had become stony again, almost unreadable, though a storm was brewing behind his eyes.

"So we will remain away from The Oasis," Amaya said, shifting her eyes away from the shattered instrument to Jeramiah. "That much we have decided on. But why stay here longer? I don't understand what more you'd want to put these people through. You've done more than enough."

Jeramiah's jaw tensed. "Maybe you're right," he said, his voice low and dangerous. "Perhaps, wherever my father's soul might be now, he might have appreciated the gesture and been satisfied with my efforts so far…" He paused and walked over to the table upon which the witch's magic knife rested. He picked it up and tilted it slowly from side to side, staring at the blade, his eyes glazing over. "But you see, Amaya… *my* soul is not satisfied. It still burns. My hunger for vengeance still disturbs my mind, and until I feel I've had it, I'm not sure I will ever be able to find peace."

Amaya let out a breath. "But Jeramiah—"

His gaze intensified. "You do realize that, had it not been for the people who inhabit this island—my own flesh and blood—my father would still be alive? I would have been able to meet him face to face, and he would be ruling over this place. I would be the prince, and my life would be full. I wouldn't have had to struggle for years trying to discover who I was… I would have an identity."

Amaya didn't argue further. She pursed her lips and fell quiet as Jeramiah resumed his prowl around the room.

When he spoke again, his voice was calmer. "Now that it appears Nuriya no longer has a hold over us, and I find myself still in The Shade—the legendary island of the Novaks—I cannot bring myself to leave now. Not yet." He gestured with a hand toward the witch. "Of course, I cannot make you stay. You've returned your favor to me already with all that you have done to help me up until now, and I could not expect you to stay longer.... Though, of course, if for old times' sake you decided to remain even for another day, I would be indebted to you."

Amaya pursed her lips as though she was seriously considering his proposal. "Well," she began slowly, "if it's just for another day or so, I will stay with you... for old times' sake." Then her eyes narrowed on the vampire. "But exactly what more do you wish to do to these people?"

Jeramiah took his time in answering. He roamed slowly back over to the table and replaced the blade. His back still turned to the witch, he replied in a whisper, "I need to end the lives of three people. Derek and Sofia Novak, and Aiden Claremont. If I can see these leaders fall, I will be able to move on. I believe that I would be able to relieve my mind from the burden of revenge, and stop living in the past."

He looked disconcertingly calm as his eyes searched Amaya's face for a response. Her complexion had paled, though she was showing no signs of faltering or withdrawing her offer of help.

"I'm confused, Jeramiah," she said. "If you wanted to end those three—Derek, Sofia and Aiden—why did you request me to target their homes with fire while they were out? Why did I not do it in the dead of night, or some other time when you were sure that they were inside, asleep? It would have been easy—they could've been scorched by now."

The vampire took a seat in the chair next to her. "The reason for that is simple," he replied, leaning closer to her. He gazed at her thoughtfully, even reaching out to tuck a stray strand of her hair behind her ear. "You see, Amaya, I could have done that. As you say, it would have been easy. But that's just the problem. It would have been too easy." He shook his head. "No. When I requested you to burn down the buildings, I had already resigned myself to the fact that I wouldn't have time to pull off their end the way I wanted it. I just satisfied myself with the knowledge that, once I'd gained more favors from Nuriya, I'd be able to return a second time to finish the job the way it should be done. But now that we find ourselves with more time, I need to end the trio who caused the most suffering to my father, in a way that does justice to him... And really, there's only one way to do that."

"What exactly are you thinking?" Amaya asked, her eyes widening.

A small smile crept across Jeramiah's lips. The way it split his pale face made him look snakelike. "I think I'll leave the exact details of their demise to the hunters. They've been incredibly patient in waiting outside the island's boundary for so long. I think it's about time someone threw them a bone… Don't you?"

Chapter 16: Ben

No. No!

My mind spiraled into a panic as Jeramiah left his seat and walked over to the mantelpiece, where he picked up an old piece of parchment and a quill.

"I need ink," he muttered, addressing the witch. He pulled up a chair and sat down at the table. Amaya manifested a bottle of black ink and planted it down on the table next to him. He dipped his quill into the ink and began to scrawl:

"Before 3 PM this afternoon, the king and queen of The Shade, along with the ex-hunter Aiden Claremont, will be waiting on the cluster of rocks southwest of your ships and outside The Shade's boundary. Be there to capture them, or ignore this

message at your own risk.

Signed,

An interested third party."

"Before 3 PM," Amaya murmured, reading the note over Jeramiah's shoulder. "That doesn't give us much time at all... And the hunters... Jeramiah, is this really the best way to do this?"

Jeramiah's face hardened. "It was the bullet of a hunter that killed my father."

I didn't know how he knew about the circumstances of his father's death—I could only assume that he had learned what had happened from the Nasiris. Somehow, he had formed the conclusion that Lucas Novak had been the victim. I didn't understand why the jinn would lead him to believe this—or perhaps they hadn't, and Jeramiah's belief was borne from the pain of losing his father—but whatever had happened, my cousin was convinced that my family were wrongdoers who needed to be destroyed. I wondered if he even knew that Lucas had been shot while attempting to murder my mother.

Amaya now looked past the point of arguing, resigned to the fact that there was no budging her vampire companion from his bloodthirsty course.

"All right... well, what would you like me to do next?" she asked.

Jeramiah folded up his note and placed the parchment in

the witch's hand. "First of all, you will deliver this to the hunters," he said. "Take it directly to the captain of any one of those ships and make sure that he sees it. Then you'll need to return to me as fast as you can."

Amaya frowned. "But if I leave the boundary, how will I reenter the island?"

"Good point," Jeramiah replied, raising a hand to his chin and stroking it. "I will swim to the boundary—in a straight line from the Port. Just make sure you're visible, and I'll spot you. I'll reach out and hopefully I'll be able to pull you back through."

"Then you will travel with me now, I assume," the witch said. "I'll transport us by magic and drop you off in the water near the boundary."

"No," Jeramiah said. "I'll head there myself… This could be my last run through the island. But don't worry. I'll make sure that you're not waiting long—if at all—for me."

She nodded, sliding the parchment beneath her sleeve. "And after that?"

Jeramiah paused before his voice lowered. "After that, we just need to ensure that the promised guests show up on time for their party."

Chapter 17: Ben

Amaya recast the invisibility spell and vanished with the note, leaving Jeramiah and me standing alone in the room.

My eyes turned on the vampire. Anger welled within me. He moved to the duo of candles sitting on the ledge by the shuttered window and snuffed them both out, plunging the room into darkness. Then he left the living area and let himself out of the front door. I hurried after him, my eyes boring into the back of his head as he stepped outside and paused briefly, drawing in a deep breath of fresh air. He gazed around the dark, empty field—at least, it was empty for him.

The moment he stepped out, the crowd of ghosts' attention shot toward him. They began to approach, keeping a distance of about five feet as they circled around him, and gazed at him expectantly. I guessed that they were all waiting for the "man with the pipe" to start playing again. As shrill as that tune sounded up close, they seemed to genuinely get pleasure from it. Perhaps I would too if I'd been a ghost as long as them.

Jeramiah ventured forward, away from the farmhouse and out onto the soil. He picked up speed and began sprinting toward the woods.

"Bastard," I cursed, running in his wake.

"Hey! What are you doing?" one of the ghosts called to me—the air stewardess, Lucinda—as I caught up with Jeramiah, but I ignored her.

My arms outstretched, I motioned to grip Jeramiah by the neck. My fingers passed through him like air. I balled up my hands into fists and tried to punch him, push him, make him stumble, do anything to slow him in his deadly race, but I was as useless as vapor.

"You're just the snake your father was," I spat, wishing to God that he could hear me.

I leveled with him as he continued running at breakneck speed. He'd now entered the woods and was whipping through the redwood trees.

I didn't know exactly how he was planning to drag my parents and grandfather out of the island. He would make the witch do it somehow. I guessed they'd catch my family when there were no other witches around. Amaya would swoop in and… *I need to warn them! But how?*

My entire being swelled with aggravation. *What is the point of this damned existence? I would be just as useful to my family if I really were dead.* The thought that I had the knowledge to prevent my parents and grandfather from becoming victims of Jeramiah's deadly plan, while being utterly unable to warn them about it, was leading me toward the brink of insanity.

3 PM. Even that time was uncertain. Jeramiah had said that my family would be taken to the rocks *before* 3 PM. *What time is it now?* I didn't even know. How long would Amaya take in delivering the message to the hunters? When would she be back, and when exactly was she going to attempt to steal away my parents and grandfather?

I attempted to bring some order to my frenzied mind, but being about two feet away from Jeramiah as he continued hurtling forward wasn't helping. His presence was only aggravating me further and making it more difficult to think clearly. I hung back and let him continue without me. It wasn't like I could do anything by following him anyway.

I had heard and seen enough. Now I had to rack my brain as to what I could possibly do. I kept moving forward, though at a slower pace as I tried to clear my mind of panic and make way for logic. But my thoughts were frozen on where

Jeramiah and Amaya were right now and what they might be doing. *Could Amaya have delivered the note already?*

Then, as I passed by the Great Dome, a light switched on and blasted through my foggy mind.

I recalled what Jeramiah had tried to do in there less than an hour ago, before my parents and their council had caused an interruption. He had asked the witch to put him into a dreamful slumber, and he had been convinced that, if Lucas still roamed the earth as a ghost, he would be able to sense his presence.

A dreamful slumber. My cousin's request played over in my head.

Thanks to my encounter with Ernest back in The Tavern, I already knew that ghosts could intercept others' dreams. They could peer into the living's bubbles of sleep as though they were peering through a window… *But could that really be a two-way window?* Was it really possible for a living, breathing person to communicate with a ghost via a dream? It seemed unbelievable but, as I reminded myself with a grimace, I wasn't exactly a stranger to fantastical occurrences. Besides, I didn't know how else Jeramiah had been expecting to be aware of Lucas's presence.

But now, I didn't have time for doubts. Time was slipping through my fingers like sand. For all I knew, Amaya could have finished her first task already and be on her way back to the boundary of the island, where Jeramiah would be waiting…

This was the only glimmer of hope I had and, as faint as it was, in my present state, trying was the only thing that I could do.

Chapter 18: Jeramiah

I'd only made it halfway to the beach when I was met with an unexpected, though by no means unwelcome, surprise. I came across Amaya in the woods.

"That was fast," I remarked, half delighted and half confused. "Why have you removed your invisibility?" I was still invisible and, if I hadn't noticed her, we would have missed each other. "And how did you get back inside the boundary without me?"

Amaya shook her head. "No," she breathed. "I haven't even made it out of this island yet. The Shade's witches have put up an extra boundary, barricading land from the ocean. I cannot even reach the waves. They must have done it as a response to the merfolk infestation. I tried to break through it, but I'm simply not strong enough. It's the combined effort of at least half a dozen witches. I lifted my invisibility spell hoping that I would come across you on my way back."

I cursed beneath my breath. Amaya hadn't been able to break through the outer boundary of the island either. Hence we had waited for Benjamin's submarine to come along in order to gain initial access to the island.

I should have considered the possibility that they would put up a second boundary. Although it had been a thrill to infest their beautiful waters with the vile sea creatures—something that hadn't been difficult to do with Amaya's beckoning potion and our ability to pull them inside—now it was working against me.

I reached up to my hair and raked my fingers through it. "Let's think," I said, breathing out slowly. "There must be a way around this."

Amaya held her breath.

"There has to be someone on this island who has permission to pass in and out," I mused. "And if anyone has that permission, who else would it be but the rulers—Derek and Sofia Novak?"

"I agree they'd be the obvious choice," Amaya replied, tight-lipped.

"So," I went on, "only a slight change of course is in

order… Our targets must be captured sooner than we had planned."

Chapter 19: Ben

A dream. I had to intercept a dream. It could be anyone's dream. I was too desperate to care. But who might be dreaming at this time of day? There had to be someone in The Shade taking an afternoon nap.

I left the Great Dome and headed toward the Residences. Though, after Kailyn's death and the fires that had shaken the island overnight, I was doubtful that any supernaturals would be sleeping. Still, it felt like the logical place to start. But as I arrived at the courtyard outside the Sanctuary where the funeral had taken place—now cleared of people, though still flooded with flowers—I stopped short.

The Sanctuary. That was where my aunt had been resting.

My now human aunt, who had just recently given birth. If anyone was likely to be taking an afternoon nap right now on this island, it would be her. Plus, she also had psychic abilities. Maybe that would make it easier for me to get through to her. I changed course abruptly and ran headfirst through the door of the witch's temple.

I hurried to the room where I had found Vivienne resting with her baby, but as I arrived outside, my heart already sank in disappointment. Two voices emanated from the bedroom—Vivienne's, and that of my uncle. I pushed my head through the door all the same, to verify that yes, she was awake, sitting upright on the bed and feeding her beautiful baby, while Xavier sat by her side and they talked in hushed tones.

Dammit.

Still, although she wasn't sleeping, Vivienne was prone to prophetic visions even when awake... Perhaps, just perhaps, she might sense me... I moved further into the room and spoke her name, walked up to her bed and tried to touch her arm; anything to get her attention. But she didn't respond in the slightest.

I had to find someone else. And fast. I resumed my original plan—head to the Residences. I darted through the trees and, once I neared within twenty feet of the burnt wreck where my parents'—and my—penthouse had once been, I lowered myself to the ground in front of a tree and leaned my back against its thick trunk.

Then I took my thoughts back in time to when I had shared a dream with Ernest. I closed my eyes, as I had done then. Slowly, I cleared the debris from my mind, even as it felt like the most impossible task in the world. Ernest had been adamant about that—that my mind be relaxed and open, to make it receptive to the minds of others.

I wasn't sure how close I had to be to a person to pick up on their dream, but as I kept my eyes sealed closed, forcing myself deeper and deeper into relaxation, I was relieved to find that it wasn't long before I encountered my first dream.

The vision of a grand hall lit by flaming torchlight trickled into my mind's eye. Its walls were covered with crimson draperies, and the chamber was bare except for a long table that ran down its center. Piled up on the table's surface was enough food to feed an army. Despite row upon row of steaming pots, there was only one seat that was taken, at the head of the table—by an ogre. A female ogre… Bella. Although there appeared to be savories aplenty—I was certain that I even spotted some fried human toes—a towering cake was set in front of her. It looked like a wedding cake—with pure white and light pink icing—and it was so high that it reached the height of her chin.

Cupping her hands, she dug both of them into the sides of

the cake at once, withdrawing two sticky handfuls. Raising one hand, she slapped its contents into her mouth…

I lifted my head and opened my eyes, shaking away the dream. *What is it with me and ogres' dreams?* I'd thought to myself that absolutely anyone would do, but something told me that competing with that cake for Bella's attention would be a losing battle.

No. I had to find someone else. But the fact that I had managed to intercept this first dream so quickly gave me hope that I wouldn't have to wait too long before another one came along… and this time, hopefully not Brett's.

I leaned my head against the bark and closed my eyes again.

My hope of finding another dream soon—and an ogre-free dream at that—was not dashed, but the second dream I came upon I spent even less time in than Bella's. It must have been the dream of either Claudia or Yuri—since those were the two figures who'd been writhing around on a silk-adorned, four-poster bed. Reminding myself that Claudia was pregnant, I guessed that it was hers. It made sense for her to be taking an afternoon nap.

Trying to forget what had just blasted through my head, I settled myself against the tree and closed my eyes again for a third time. Hopefully, this time would be lucky.

I saw nothing but blackness for the next five minutes, or at least what felt like five minutes. I was beginning to feel tense, wondering if it had been a grave mistake to dismiss the previous two dreams so quickly. Perhaps I should have tried to communicate while I'd had the chance. I had just taken it for granted that a third one wouldn't be far away... And then it arrived. A third vision took over my consciousness.

Stretching out all around me was a dark ocean, its waves glistening beneath a starry night sky. The moon was full, and roaming along the beach was a lone figure. It was our beach—The Shade's beach, just near the port—and the figure... the figure was River.

Would she really be sleeping at this time? Last I knew, the humans were not aware of the devastation from last night. That would not have kept her up worrying. And the last time I had seen her, she had certainly looked worn out and tired.

She was wrapped up in a thick shawl which she held close to her chest as she gazed out into the distance. Her eyes were fixed intently on a spot above the waves. As I followed her gaze, I realized what she was staring at—the shiny roof of a submarine, partially visible in the water. It was moving quickly toward the shore—so fast it was almost as though the vessel possessed supernatural speed. It arrived at the Port and stopped by the jetty. River's breathing quickened. She ran toward it. As the hatch opened, a head of dark hair emerged above the roof.

"Ben!" she shouted.

It was a man climbing out of the submarine and as he turned around to face her… the man was me. The other me's face lit up as River closed the distance between the two of us and she threw herself at me. I stared as my lips locked with hers, my arms engulfing her small waist and pulling her flush against me. My hands moved up her body and into her thick, dark hair as we kissed with all the passion of a newly-wedded couple.

"River," the other me said, detaching my lips from hers to catch a breath.

Tears burned in the corners of her eyes even as she smiled. She buried her head against my chest and whispered, "I was afraid, Ben. So afraid. I thought that you might never return. How are you, and what took you so long?"

"I'm okay," the other me replied, cupping her face in my hands. "I was away a long time because the Elder was stubborn. But I'm finally rid of him. Everything is all right now."

Those last words coming from my mouth grated on my nerves.

"No!" I shouted. "Everything is not all right!"

There was a stunned silence, and to my shock, River turned round around to face me. The real me. I wasn't sure what I'd expected to happen—I'd shouted more out of frustration than anything else. But now she gazed at me, her eyes wide and her face twisted with confusion. She looked from me to the second me and then back again. Then the second me evaporated.

"Ben?" she breathed, gaping at me as though she had seen… a ghost.

She moved toward me across the sand, slowly and cautiously, as one might approach an alien. She reached a hand tentatively up to my face, and… I felt her. Her fingers against my jaw. Her soft touch. I reached up my hand and closed it around hers. I was able to hold her hand.

Taken by this revelation that a ghost could feel in dreams—even if it was just the illusion of feeling—I dipped my head down and pushed my lips against hers. Her breath hitched, and then her arms wrapped around my neck, pulling me in closer as my tongue parted her lips.

I lost myself in the moment, relishing her touch. Touch I'd thought that I might never be able to experience again… But although I could've continued kissing River for hours, or however long her dream lasted, I had to tear our lips apart.

She gazed deep into my eyes. Her beautiful features were still marred with a frown.

"Which one is you?" she whispered, casting her eyes over her shoulder to where the second me had emerged from the submarine and stood with her near the jetty.

"This is me," I assured her, gripping her head in my hands and planting a firm kiss against her forehead. "I promise."

My hands slid down her shoulders and gripped her hard.

"You must listen to me," I said, my eyes boring into hers. "My parents and grandfather are in danger. Jeramiah is on the island with the witch, Amaya. He's planning to round up all three, take them to the cluster of rocks—near The Shade's port, but outside the boundary— and hand all three over to the hunters. You need to warn them urgently. He could strike anytime between now and 3PM."

Her eyes filled with fear as they shot back over her shoulder toward the dark island.

I forced her attention back to me. "You must tell them to stay near witches at all times, and they need to smoke Jeramiah and the witch out of The Shade. His base was in the old farmhouse near the potato fields. I don't know if he'll return to that house, but there is a chance that he might. The two have been roaming the island beneath the protection of an invisibility spell, but you've got to find them."

River nodded fiercely, even as she looked panicked. "O-Okay," she said. "I'll go right now! You should come with me, too!"

"You need to wake up, River," I said. I pushed my mouth against hers in a short, passionate kiss. "Wake up. Wake up now."

"But your parents!" she exclaimed, glancing again at the island. She took a step back and, gripping my hand, began attempting to race toward the Port. "There's no time to lose."

"Yes, but you have to wake up first."

I reeled her in and pulled her against me, even as she tried to keep moving forward. I clutched her shoulders and shook them hard, harder than I would have liked to, but I reminded myself this was just a dream. And I had to jolt her into wakefulness. If I let her go wandering off, she would only keep dreaming.

Finally, my firmness worked. The scene around me faded away, along with River, and the feel of her shoulders in my hands. Now, with my eyes still closed, all I saw was blackness. River's dream had ended.

Chapter 20: Ben

My eyes shot open. I looked around, my consciousness returning to the dark forest surrounding me.

Now that River was awake, I had to pray that firstly, she would remember the dream, and secondly, she would find it in herself to act on it. Sane people didn't act on dreams. Why would they when dreams were, for the most part, nonsensical fabrications of the subconscious? I had to hope that, somehow, River would be able to sense that this dream was different. That I had infected her with my urgency.

I left my spot beneath the tree and began to race toward the Vale. Dashing along the streets, and arriving outside River and her family's townhouse, I walked through the closed front door. As I entered the hallway, I heard voices coming from the kitchen at the end of the corridor.

I hurried through a second closed door to see Jamil and Nadia— who looked much better than when I'd seen her earlier— sitting around the kitchen table, bowls of pasta in front of them, while River stood leaning against the counter. She wore the same day clothes she had changed into earlier. Were it not for her mussed hair and bleary eyes, I wouldn't have been able to tell that she had just taken a nap. She had dark circles under her eyes, and she barely looked more refreshed than the last time I'd seen her.

I walked up to her and tried to take her hands in mine, as I would've been able to do in the dream. As my fingers drifted right through her, I stared down at her, watching every expression that crossed her face intently.

Come on, River. Come on. Remember what I told you.

She reached a hand up and clamped it around her shoulder before rolling her neck slowly. There was a restlessness about her demeanor, and that gave me hope.

"I didn't mean to doze off, actually," River murmured.

"You needed it, honey," her mother said, eyeing her with concern. "Go sleep some more if you're tired."

River shook her head. "No," she said. She left the counter and took a seat at the table, opposite Jamil.

"Won't you eat something?" Nadia asked.

"Maybe a bit later," River replied vaguely. She breathed out, leaning her elbows on the table and rubbing her fingers against her forehead. "I had a strange dream," she admitted finally.

That's it. Come on, River.

"What was it?" Jamil asked, glancing up curiously from his food.

"I saw Ben again… two Bens actually. One of them arrived back on the island in a submarine, and assured me that he was fine. But the other… he looked so pale, so ethereal. He told me that Jeramiah was on the island. He said that Jeramiah managed to get through the boundary with his witch companion, Amaya. And he said that Derek, Sofia and Aiden are in danger from the duo."

She paused, looking from her brother to her mother for their reactions.

"That was the whole dream?" her mother asked.

"That was the gist of it… it ended with Ben shaking me and urging me to wake up. And then I did." She released another breath, looking unnerved.

"Dreams can be the strangest things," Nadia muttered, spooning pasta into her mouth.

"Come on, River!" I said, out loud this time.

Silence fell between the three of them.

"I mean," River continued, "it was just a dream, but…

isn't it strange how I woke up just when he told me to? It was like I actually felt his urgency. I woke up in a panic, and I was sweating."

"Why don't you go talk to Derek and Sofia?" Jamil suggested, eyeing his sister, his fork paused mid-air. "Since they returned from their journey, you've wanted to go see them anyway, haven't you?"

I couldn't have felt more grateful to a person than I did to Jamil Giovanni in that moment.

River nodded. "Yes. I am going to go and talk to them. Now."

Thank God.

Now, River, you need to hurry. You need to run like you've never run—

She got up from the table and headed for the door.

"Well," her mother called after her, "there's lots of food waiting for you when you return."

"Thanks," River murmured. She reached the front door and pulled on a pair of boots.

"Where are you going?" Lalia called from what sounded like the sitting room.

"I'll be back soon," River replied as she closed the door behind her.

Emerging on the street outside, she looked right and left. I was glad that she chose to take a left and headed toward the town square. That would be the quickest route out of the town. I hoped that by now, even though she hadn't been on the island all that long, she knew her way around well enough to find my parents. As she left the borders of the Vale and entered the thick forest, she sped up into a sprint, whipping almost as fast as a vampire through the trees. But even as she hurtled forward, I wished that she would move faster.

When she approached the Residences and arrived at the foot of the tree where my and my parents' penthouse had once been, she gazed up toward the burnt tree tops and let out a gasp of horror.

"Oh, my…" she mouthed.

She gazed all around the area before her eyes fixed on the neighboring tree. I guessed that she was about to climb up to find out what happened when footsteps crunched behind us.

It was Rose and Caleb approaching.

"Rose," River called. She hurried up to my sister. River cast her eyes upward again at the treetops before returning to Rose. "What on earth happened here?"

My sister's face was blanched. "There was a fire," she said, her voice several tones deeper than usual. "Both here and in my grandfather's mountain cabin. My parents are okay, and so is Aiden… but his girlfriend, Kailyn… she didn't make it."

"Oh, God… And you don't know how the fires started?"

"Lucas' demon son," I hissed.

"We're not sure," Rose replied. "My father is launching an investigation as we speak."

"Where is your father?" River asked.

"In the Great Dome, along with my mom and the rest of The Shade's council."

"I need to speak with your parents." River's face had drained of all color. "I just had a dream involving Ben. He told me that Jeramiah was on this island, that somehow Jeramiah managed to gain entrance and he's targeting your father, mother and grandfather. Oh, God."

Rose looked bewildered, but I was relieved when she didn't delay River with any questions. She reached out and grabbed River's hand. "Come with me," she said. The three of them turned on their heel and began to dash through the woods.

Hurrying after them, I found myself running side by side with Caleb, who was about the same height as me.

"How long ago did you have this dream?" he asked River as they ran.

"Just now," River replied breathlessly. "Like ten or fifteen minutes ago."

Caleb's expression darkened. Silence fell between the three, and none of them exchanged another word until they arrived outside the Great Dome. Caleb was the first to reach the entrance. He clutched the handle and pushed open the heavy door. It caused a loud creak and as the three of them burst into the meeting room, all eyes turned on them. I was relieved to see my mother and father sitting at the head of the table, but when I scanned the room in search of my grandfather, I couldn't spot him.

"River needs to talk to you urgently," Rose said, still clutching River's hand. She led her up to my parents at the head of the table.

As my father stood up, his imposing form towering over her, River looked rather intimidated to be standing before The Shade's king, though she began to explain in a surprisingly steady voice. "I think I know who is behind this. I believe that Jeramiah 'Stone' Novak is on this island with a witch. He's targeting you, your wife, and Aiden."

So stark was the silence that followed, it was as though someone had hit the mute button.

My parents gaped at River.

"What brings you to this conclusion?" my father asked.

At this, River faltered a little. "I–I had a dream. Just now. Ben was in it. He told me that his cousin was on the island, that I needed to urgently warn you to keep witches near you to protect you at all times. He also said that Jeramiah was staying in an old farmhouse, the one near the potato fields?"

A hundred questions crowded behind my parents' eyes but, seeing River's earnestness, they turned to face the others. "You know that old house." My father's voice boomed through the chamber. "Search the building and its surrounding area immediately."

The council shot to their feet and began piling out of the hall.

"Do you know where Aiden is?" River asked, her eyes filling with worry as they trailed along the line of people leaving the room.

My mother's face tensed. "He didn't attend the meeting," she said. "Last I saw of him, he was sitting by the lake. He just wanted to be alone."

"We need to locate him at once," my father said. He turned to Ibrahim and Corrine, who had hung back from the crowd. "Will you two accompany us?"

"Of course, Derek," Ibrahim replied.

"I'll go search for Aiden, if you like," Corrine offered. "That will free the rest of you up to join the hunt."

"Yes," my father said. "Please do that, Corrine."

The witch gave him a curt nod, and then vanished.

My father glanced again at River before addressing Ibrahim. "This could be nothing but a fabrication of River's imagination, but I'm not about to take the risk that it isn't."

"I have no idea why I had the dream," River said, her expression still mired with confusion, "or why on earth I dreamed Ben telling me all this, but… I didn't even find out about your penthouse or Aiden's mountain cabin burning down until after I woke up. It just seems like too much of a coincidence."

"I agree," my father murmured, even as he began hurrying to the Dome's exit. "And even if it does turn out to be a wild coincidence," he continued once they'd piled outside, "no harm's ever done by taking extra precautions."

With that, everyone formed a circle around Ibrahim and they vanished. They would no doubt join the others in the fields. Satisfied that, thanks to my love, River, everyone had received sufficient warning, I was now burning to locate Jeramiah and the witch again. Ever since I'd lost sight of them, not knowing where exactly they were on the island had been eating away at me. I prayed that Corrine would soon find my grandfather, and they hadn't managed to swipe him already. He had been all alone and vulnerable by the lake...

I tried to stop thinking about the worst-case scenario, and focus on what I had to do next.

I need to think. When I parted ways with them, Amaya had left to deliver Jeramiah's note to the hunters, while the vampire was supposed to follow soon after her. His plan had been to wait just within the boundary, and then assist Amaya back in once she had successfully completed her task.

Now the question was, had they already managed to complete the first part of their plan?

Truth be told, I'd expected it to take longer to raise the

alarm around the island—and that was if I'd even managed it at all. But it had not taken much time for the idea of intercepting dreams to occur to me, and then the dreams themselves had been fast in coming. And now, thanks to River's receptiveness, warning the others had gone smoothly.

I was uncertain if enough time had passed for Amaya to deliver the note to one of the vessel's captains. Hopefully, the witch was still hovering near the naval ships, while my cousin waited in the waves by the boundary for her return. Jeramiah and Amaya still being outside the island would have been the best possible thing that could happen. But there was only one way to know for sure.

Chapter 21: Ben

I swept across the island and quickly arrived at the beach. I dashed across the sand, and when I reached the water I continued running over the surface of the waves. I had been onshore for some time now, and although the sensation was no different to traveling on land, the thought of running on water had become strange to me again.

I directed my gaze toward the boundary, praying that I would see Jeramiah's dark head bobbing above the waves. He had said that he would swim in a direct line from the Port, and that was exactly where I headed, but when I arrived, to my dismay I couldn't see him anywhere.

I scanned the surrounding water, just in case he had drifted further along. Heck, I was so desperate that I traveled several miles left and right along the boundary. Still, I couldn't spot him. Unless Jeramiah had dallied to enjoy the scenery on his way to the shore and hadn't even reached the beach yet—which I couldn't bring myself to believe—this could only mean that he and Amaya had returned to the island and were now preparing for the second part of their plan.

I stopped my futile patrol over the waves and shifted my focus back to the island. My task had become significantly more difficult. They could be anywhere in The Shade now. Where would I look first?

Everyone was searching the area near the farmhouse, but as Jeramiah and his witch were invisible, it wouldn't be difficult to dodge the searchers. The raiding of the old building would be useful for my parents to verify River's dream, because on arriving there they would find the makeshift stone that Jeramiah had crafted in honor of his father—assuming that my cousin had not returned to the building and removed it already.

Now that I was certain Jeramiah was back on the island, the first thing I needed to do was return to the fields and check that my parents were okay. Yes, I had managed to warn them to be on their guard, but Jeramiah and the witch still had the advantage of being invisible. I could see through their invisibility, and I had not noticed them near the Great Dome while the meeting was taking place, so I couldn't be sure if Jeramiah had been aware of their location or knew that they were now headed to the farmhouse... And where was my grandfather?

I hurried to the shore and headed as fast as I could back toward the vegetable fields. On approaching the courtyard outside the Sanctuary, as much as I was in a desperate hurry, something caught my eye and I stopped still. Lying on the ground near a barrowful of wilted flowers were two of our witches.

For a fearful moment I thought that they might have even been dead, but on nearing, I could see that they were breathing. They were sound asleep.

From the way they both lay strewn near the barrow, it looked like they might have been in the midst of tidying up after the funeral.

Oh, God.

Tearing my eyes away from the witches' sleeping forms, I continued hurtling forward. A hundred alarm bells rang out in every corner of my mind, and as I stumbled across a group of human children—perhaps six or seven years of age—lying asleep in the undergrowth beside wooden swords and hand catapults, my alarm only grew louder.

As I made it out of the woods and approached the fields, I beheld a scene I'd feared I might find.

Scattered about the field surrounding the farmhouse were dozens of sleeping forms—The Shade's council members.

No. No!

The only signs of life, in this field, ironically, came from the ghosts who still hovered by the old building.

I scanned the ground desperately for my parents, but I couldn't see them. I approached the farmhouse, ignoring Lucinda as she called to me. I swept through the house in a panic.

It was empty. The memorial stone was missing, and so were my parents.

I stormed out of the house and back into the field. I raced up to Lucinda and tried to grab her, forgetting for the hundredth damn time in my urgency that my hands were made of nothing.

"What happened here?" I demanded.

"The crowd of people came," she murmured, raising her eyebrows as she gazed around at the sleeping bodies surrounding us. "Rather strange people if you ask me… They were looking around the area, and they seemed particularly interested in the farmhouse. Then it was like they all had a heart attack at once. They fell to the ground and now are apparently sleeping. Then I spotted the man with the pipe. He came here with his lady friend. They picked up two people, and then they both just… vanished." She looked utterly confused even as she said the words. Although she was a ghost, I guessed that she had not had many encounters with other types of supernaturals.

I didn't bother asking which two people Jeramiah had swooped down on.

And where is my grandfather? Have they caught him already?

Amaya must have cast a sleeping spell over the island to wipe out any obstacles our witches might pose. Being able to affect the whole island like this meant that she was more skilled a witch than I had expected.

Although I was raring to go racing after Jeramiah and Amaya to the cluster of rocks, to see what state my parents and grandfather were in, what use would it do? I had to get help. I had to wake someone!

I scanned the ground, and my eyes fell on River and Rose, who'd fallen and lay sleeping next to each other on the soil. There were others that I could've approached, but I instinctively moved closer to River. She had already helped me the first time, it should be both easier and faster to get through to her a second time… I just had to hope that the slumber Amaya had cast upon everyone did not preclude dreams.

I knelt on the soil next to her and closed my eyes, squeezing them tightly shut and trying to clear my mind.

The minutes that followed were agonizing, just sitting

there in the quiet field, shrouded in darkness with my eyes closed.

Then, as I was beginning to give up hope that even a single person in the field was dreaming, I caught a glimpse of stars twinkling behind my eyelids. A vision emerged, a vision of a night sky. The moon was nowhere to be seen, but the brightness of the stars almost made up for its absence. Calm waves rolled beneath the star-strewn canvas, and floating in the midst of them was River.

She was lying on her back, sleeping, with an expression of profound peace on her face.

"River," I called. "River, wake up."

I descended on her in the dream, reaching out to grip her shoulders. I squeezed and shook her, just as hard as I'd done in her previous dream, but this time, she wasn't budging.

Wake up, River.

For the love of God, wake up!

Chapter 22: Derek

Consciousness trickled slowly through my brain. My head ached dully. My limbs felt stiff and rigid. An odd warmth touched my skin. My heavy eyelids parted and I found myself assaulted by a blinding light. I was forced to clamp them shut and reopen them more slowly. I squinted, allowing my pupils to adjust to the change in brightness. I found myself staring up at a sun-streaked sky.

I tried to sit up, but my limbs would not obey my brain. I could only move my neck and the muscles in my face. I turned my head to my left to see Sofia lying next to me. On her other side lay Aiden. Both appeared to be in deep slumber. Sea spray wet my face and I realized that we were lying on a cluster of craggy rocks, surrounding by rolling waves. I recognized these rocks—they served as a landmark for our island's boundary.

I wasn't sure how long we'd been lying here. I guessed it couldn't have been that long because, although Sofia and Aiden's vampire skin had begun to singe, neither was too badly wounded yet. It wouldn't be long though before their skin started to flake and peel away. A panic welled within me. Why weren't they waking up? The pain should have aroused them by now. The only comfort I had was that they were still breathing.

"Sofia." I spoke up, my voice crackling through my dry throat. "Aiden."

Since I'd opened my eyes, my memory had been trickling back to me in pieces, and now the puzzle was complete. Sofia and I had been searching inside the farmhouse when an overwhelming sleepiness had come upon me. I hadn't even had a chance to fight it before my eyes closed. I was sure that I'd fallen asleep before I even hit the floor.

"Uncle." A voice spoke. A deep male voice. A voice that sparked a chill at the back of my neck. It sounded eerily familiar.

I strained to see who had spoken, but although it came from only a few feet away, a rock near my head blocked my view. Then I didn't need to strain myself. A man holding a wide umbrella leapt on top of the rock and gazed down at me.

So this is Jeramiah Novak. My nephew. He looked less like his father then I'd expected—with long, dark hair tied up in a bun—although he shared the same cold, harsh eyes and hard, square jawline. He certainly had the height and build of a Novak, too.

I glared up at him, uncertain of how even to respond. *Hello? Nice to finally meet you?* I knew almost nothing about this man, while he had never met me, and yet he stared down at me with such hatred that one would have thought I'd been his enemy all his life.

"Nephew," I replied in kind, clenching my jaw.

He leapt from the rock and landed near my head, still gazing down at me with a calm expression on his face, though his eyes glinted dangerously. I knew those eyes. I'd seen them before in my own brother. They were the eyes of a man who had nothing to lose.

"I'll admit," I said, glaring daggers up at him, "this is not the way I'd hoped our first meeting would go."

His lips parted slowly from the hard line they had formed. "On the contrary, this is exactly how I'd imagined it." I could see that he was being careful not to cast any of the shadow from his umbrella upon us.

Sofia began to stir. Her eyes lifted open and she grimaced, then groaned in pain. She couldn't even turn over on her stomach to at least hide her face from the sun.

Time was running out for Sofia and Aiden. The clock had started ticking the moment Jeramiah had placed them in the sun. While one thing was abundantly clear—I had to maintain my calm around this vampire—it was hard with my wife and father-in-law being tortured just a few feet away from me.

Even I, in my human form, found the sun's blaze to be unpleasant. There were no clouds at all in the sky, and although midday had come and gone, the sun was still glaringly bright.

As my eyes shifted back to my nephew, his stubborn jaw locked, I was struck by a wave of déjà vu. It had been almost twenty years now since I'd had to deal with my brother, but now, as his son stood over me, I found myself sliding into exactly the same mode I had always tried to assume with him. While Lucas had been the one to try to spark an argument or fight, I had tried to avoid it—it was only when he'd pushed my hand too far that I'd snapped. I realized that I needed to take the same approach with his son, who appeared to be made of the same fabric.

Lucas had reveled in conflict and evoking a reaction in me. I wasn't going to give the latter to Jeramiah, and I was going to do all that I could to avoid the former.

"And what else did you imagine for this meeting?" I asked,

maintaining a steady voice.

As though he had not heard my question, Jeramiah glanced away from me and fixed his gaze on Aiden, who, like Sofia, was also just beginning to come to. He left my side and walked over to him.

"Amaya," Jeramiah called.

A witch appeared from nowhere and stood by my nephew's side. She was tall and thin, with sleek black hair and sharp, elongated facial features.

"Keep me in shadow," he ordered.

She took the umbrella from him and held it up over him.

Now, with both hands free, he bent down and gripped Aiden by the throat. Aiden—his eyes still drowning in mourning over the loss of his lover—grunted, unable to fight back, as Jeramiah lifted him up and pinned him upright against the side of the rock.

"No!" Sofia gasped. "Let go of him!"

Jeramiah turned his back on us and I could only imagine the expression on his face as he stared at Aiden Claremont.

Just like Lucas. He never was interested in a fair fight.

The way he was holding Aiden reminded me of the way Lucas had once held Sofia—helpless and pinned up against a wall—while he had assaulted her in my Sun Room.

"Pray tell, vampire," I spoke up, even as it was becoming increasingly difficult to maintain an even tone, "what exactly are you seeking to accomplish by all this? Apparently not a family reunion…"

Jeramiah threw a cold glance over his shoulder at me, and this time, his poker face broke and a scowl spread across his stony features.

I wasn't sure exactly what was going through his mind as his hold abruptly loosened on Aiden, causing him to collapse onto the sharp rocks, but I was glad that at least I had managed to cause a distraction—however fleeting it might be.

At this point, it felt like I was dancing on hot coals, trying to figure out how to get through to a man I'd never met, going solely by the instincts I had developed while dealing with my brother.

He returned to my side and bent down, his knees jutting out and almost knocking my shoulder. Amaya followed him, continuing to provide shade.

His sharp blue eyes fixed on mine, and I held his gaze, unflinching.

"A family reunion would have been welcome, actually," he said, in a softer voice than I had expected from him. A voice that didn't quite match up with the harshness of his gaze. A voice that even quivered, ever so slightly. Perhaps he was not as closed off from emotion as he made himself out to be.

"In fact," he continued, clearing his throat, "it's what I had been hoping for the day I discovered that I was not the first

Novak to be turned into a bloodsucker." His jaw twitched. "I suppose you can imagine my disappointment when I discovered that my father had been murdered by a member of my own extended family."

"You never met your father," I stated, knowing it for a fact. I was sure that Lucas himself had been oblivious to fathering Jeramiah, and I even found myself wondering whether this young man had been the only child born from one of Lucas's many old flames. "And you were not present the day he died," I continued. "Do you know why he was killed? Do you know even the slightest thing about the circumstances of his death? Or anything about who he was during his life?"

To my surprise, a small smile curved Jeramiah's lips. Not one of amusement, but one of bitterness.

"I know more about my father than you ever bothered to find out," he said, his voice dropping to a low hiss.

A pain stabbed my chest as Sofia and Aiden's groans intensified. I didn't know where all this talking would lead, or how much longer Jeramiah would stand being distracted from what he was planning to do with us, but right now, keeping him in conversation was the only thing that I could think to do.

"Why don't you enlighten me then?" I said, a part of me genuinely curious as to what conception—or rather misconception—this vampire had formed about my brother.

"It's a bit late for that now, don't you think?" he replied. My gut twisted as he stood up. I had been hoping to keep him kneeling down on the ground, away from my wife and father-in-law.

"Jeramiah," Sofia breathed out, even as her face continued to contort with pain. She would've been writhing around by now had she had control of her limbs. "Lucas Novak was a disturbed man."

To put it politely… I thought.

"We never set out to make an enemy out of him. Since the day I arrived in The Shade, he had it in for me. He murdered an innocent girl who was staying in Derek's quarters—she was only one of his helpless victims—and he would've done the same to me. We never wanted to isolate or cause harm to him. He did both of these things to himself. He was blinded by envy of Derek and—"

"Silence!" Jeramiah's demeanor had turned to ice. Every part of his body was rigid, and his breathing had become uneven, his chest and shoulders heaving.

Sofia had overstepped the mark in what he was willing to hear about his father, it seemed. Whatever picture Jeramiah had painted for himself about my brother's character, it was obviously filled with rainbows and unicorns. And he wasn't willing to shatter his illusion.

As I gazed up into his face, now contorted with anger, it

was clear that there were many layers to this man, one of which was instability. And for that, I couldn't blame him. From what Ben had told me of his childhood, it had been traumatic, no doubt. He'd never met his father, not even once—Lucas had turned from human to vampire soon after Jeramiah's conception, and then he'd been long gone. And then Jeramiah had lost his mother when he was very young, and I couldn't imagine that his life with his grandparents had been a satisfying one, since he'd left them at such a young age to go traipsing halfway across the globe.

I guessed that my nephew had never truly felt firm ground beneath his feet. He'd never had a figurehead, or a role model.

Or perhaps he had… in his father.

Perhaps he had taken refuge in his father, and that was why he clung so tightly to his rosy vision of him, however misguided it was.

The irony was, if he weren't so bent against us, I would have invited him into our family, perhaps even treated him as though he were my own son. Since I'd first found out about Jeramiah's existence from Ben, I'd known that I never wanted to make an enemy out of him. I'd known that if I ever got the chance to meet him, I would try to hold no prejudices against him. Because I'd never been happy with the relationship—or rather lack of it—that I'd had with my brother. Jeramiah was my own flesh and blood, and he would have been welcomed onto our island. Perhaps he didn't know it—and perhaps he didn't care—but by accosting us like this, he was cutting his nose off to spite his face.

As I stared up into his angry eyes, the small amount of hope I'd held that I might still be able to turn him around and make him see sense evaporated. He didn't want the truth. He wanted anything but the truth. And if he wasn't willing to even hear us out, there was nothing we could do to try to cobble together a relationship.

Sofia and I could have gone on, kept talking, forced him to listen to what had actually happened, but it was clear that it would only aggravate him further, and I doubted we would be any better off for it.

I feared that Jeramiah was going to head back over to Aiden and continue harassing him. But, to my surprise, he didn't. He didn't walk over to Sofia either. With the witch following behind him, he moved away from us and straightened, his eyes fixing on the ocean somewhere in the distance—out of my limited angle of vision.

And then I heard it, coming from somewhere in the distance. The sound of a motor. A loud, powerful motor. It sounded like that of a speedboat.

Jeramiah turned to face us again with a much calmer expression. "I hope you don't mind," he said in a deep, low voice. "While you were asleep, we took the liberty of inviting some guests to our rendezvous. You get along with hunters, don't you?"

Chapter 23: River

"Wake up, River. Wake up." A deep voice echoed in my head. It was a familiar voice, though, buried in the depths of my subconscious, I couldn't quite put a name to it. I couldn't put a name to much at all, even myself. My being was infused with the enjoyment of a profoundly satisfying sleep.

"Wake up!" it called again.

But my sleep was too comfortable. I felt warm and deliciously relaxed. I was floating across an endless mass of gentle waves. The water lapped against the sides of my body like a massage, only serving to deepen my relaxation.

"Wake up, River!"

"No. I don't want to wake up. Go away," I thought to the

echo, irritated at the disturbance.

I tried to block the voice out. I tried to ignore it and hope that it would go away. But it only grew louder and louder, shattering my peace like a foghorn.

"Wake up!"

"Why should I wake up?" I shot back. *"There's nothing worth waking up for."*

But the voice remained persistent, each call drawing me further and further away from sleep until I was pulled back to consciousness enough that I felt damp soil beneath me. My eyelids unglued. My vision was hazy as I fought to brush away the cobwebs of sleep.

I was… in a field. The same field I'd been in just… how long ago? How could I have fallen asleep here and…

My eyes traveled over the many sleeping members of Derek and Sofia's council on the ground surrounding me. Rose slept next to me.

The atmosphere was so quiet, I could distinctly pick up the rolling of the waves on the beach.

What happened here?

I stumbled to my feet and bent down over Rose. Gripping her shoulders, I shook her hard. She didn't respond at all, and had she not been breathing, I might even have feared that she was dead. I cast my eyes over the others and tried to wake Caleb, who lay nearby. He too was still as a rock. I tried several others—some vampires I didn't even know the names of—before I straightened, panic lighting up my brain. Derek and Sofia were absent. Though the last thing I remembered, they had been in the farmhouse…

I hurried into the old building only to find that it was empty. I scanned the fields outside once more, just to double-check that Derek and Sofia definitely weren't there—that I hadn't accidentally overlooked them. They weren't.

Oh, God. How long have Derek and Sofia been missing? And where is Aiden? Did Corrine even manage to find him?

What do I do now?

One option was to keep trying to wake others up so they could assist me, but I'd just tried that. And they were all so deep in sleep that something told me that even if I stayed there shaking people for another hour, I still wouldn't have managed to arouse anyone. I had already shaken them hard—as hard as I dared to shake a person. I didn't understand how I was able to wake up and they weren't. But now was no time to ponder over it.

A witch must have been behind this. And who else but Jeramiah's witch?

My pounding heart rising to my throat, I tore my eyes away from the sleeping bodies scattered in the fields and back toward the entrance of the woods.

A chill ran down my spine as I began to race with all the

speed my legs could muster into the woods. I was still oblivious to the time, and for all I knew, it could be too late for Ben's family already. Jeramiah and Amaya had already swooped down to put everyone in a slumber. They would've grabbed Derek and Sofia, and if they'd taken them, I was sure that they would have managed to find Aiden by now too. The question was, were they still alive?

In the dream when Ben had come to me, he'd said that Jeramiah was planning to hand them over to the hunters, and that he was going to meet them on a cluster of rocks near the boundary of The Shade. But where was that exactly? As I tried to rack my brain for the location, I soon realized that the location was the least of my worries. How was I going to get there? Even if I did manage it somehow, what would I find there? Would I be in any position at all to help them, assuming they could still be helped?

My mind turned to my own family, wondering if they too had been put to sleep or whether it was just us near the farmhouse, since we'd been near Amaya's targets, Derek and Sofia.

I couldn't see a reason why Amaya would cast a spell over the human population, but now wasn't the time to find out. My family wasn't the target, Ben's was.

As I raced through the trees, winding along the forest path, I wasn't comforted to find a group of children lying sound asleep on the ground. They had wooden toys around them, and had clearly been in the middle of playing. Even these innocent children had been affected by the spell.

I feared that everyone in the island might've been hit. Then again, this island was big, and I hadn't yet ventured far from the fields. Would the witch really have bothered to cast such a wide spell? I wondered if she was even powerful enough to achieve such scope.

I still didn't know this island well, but I knew it well enough to be able to sense that the furthest point away from the agricultural area—where I guessed the spell would've been concentrated—was the Black Heights. The mountains were all the way on the other side of the island. If I hurried there, I could see if anybody at all was awake and could help…

I was tempted to just get in a boat and try to navigate there myself but, firstly, as much as I had observed Ben during our voyage across the seas, I didn't know how to work a vessel by myself. And secondly, a second boundary had been put up around the island by the witches to protect The Shade's inhabitants from the merfolk infestation. And unlike the original boundary, this one didn't allow people out, unless they had special permission. Derek and Sofia would have that, no doubt, but I certainly didn't.

And so, as I neared the clearing before the Port, I didn't head toward the jetty. I took a left turn and continued running through the forest toward the mountains.

On my way, I spotted dozens more vampires and even humans lying asleep in the woods, and even as I passed by the Vale, I couldn't hear the usual bustle of the town—it sounded eerily quiet, confirming my fears.

Still, I clung on to my thread of hope and didn't let up my speed until I arrived at the foot of the Black Heights. My eyes traveled around the mountain cabins perched among the rocks. Spotting the burnt-down cabin of Aiden and Kailyn, I shuddered. All seemed quiet—I couldn't spot anybody walking around up there—though I tried to comfort myself that did not necessarily mean they were all asleep.

Still, my eyes lowered from the cabins and I focused instead on the entrance to the mountain caves—apparently once used as storage chambers, and now carved out into exquisite apartments for the island's dragon population.

I had not ventured in here since arriving. In fact, I hadn't had much contact at all with the dragons. They kept to themselves. I realized that if anyone could help me, they would be a good bet. I just had to hope that the sleeping spell hadn't reached them.

I approached the heavy door carved into the base of the mountain, and, pushing against it, I was relieved that it wasn't locked. It ground open, allowing me entrance into a lantern-lit tunnel. The moment I stepped inside, a wonderful surge of warmth rushed through me. Although the walls, floors and ceilings were made of stone, it was as though they had some kind of central heating system behind them. They radiated heat that penetrated my skin and eased the aching of my bones—aching that I had gotten so used to by now, I took it for granted.

A heady scent of frankincense and myrrh laced the atmosphere as I traveled along the tunnel until it opened up into a grand entrance hall. The floors were made of shiny black marble, rich velvet drapes covered the walls and a grand chandelier hung in the center of the room, casting soft, orange light. When I took a left, it led to a wide corridor, just as beautifully decorated.

As my gaze traveled along it, there were carved wooden doors on either side—entrances to the various dragons' apartments, I could only assume. I headed toward the nearest door to me on my right and pressed my ear against it. I sensed movement coming from within. I let out a sigh of relief. Amaya's spell had not extended as far as I'd feared it might.

I balled my hands into fists and banged against the door. Once, twice, thrice.

Footsteps approached, and the door swung open. My eyes widened at the sheer size of the brown-haired, grey-eyed man standing in front of me. I was sure that I'd seen this dragon shifter before—though I couldn't recall his name—but up close like this, he was far more formidable. He personified strength and it looked like he could easily crush the bones in my hand if he shook it too tightly.

"I am sorry to disturb you," I said. My throat felt parched from the heat his bronzed body was exuding. "I need help urgently. The king and queen, and I think Aiden also, have been captured by an enemy. I know where they might be, but please, I need you to help me get off this island—there's a cluster of rocks just outside the boundary where they're supposed to have been taken. I'm not sure if they're still there but… Can you please help?"

The man's brows furrowed as he tightened his satin robe around him and stepped out into the corridor.

"The king and queen are in danger? We must leave once. Jeriad!" he bellowed, his baritone voice booming off the walls. "Neros! Azaiah!"

More footsteps sounded behind doors nearby, and they swung open. Out stepped three more dragon shifters. One of them, with wavy black hair that licked the sides of his face—Jeriad, I believed his name was—looked even larger and more intimidating than the one who stood in front of me. All were dressed casually, in cotton pants and loose shirts.

"What is it, Ridan?" Jeriad asked, sauntering toward him.

"The king, queen and Aiden are in danger!" I replied for Ridan. "I can explain along the way, but we must hurry out of the boundary! Do you know how we could do that, since the witches put up a second one—?"

"Yes, we know," Jeriad said, his piercing aquamarine eyes falling on me. "There is an area on the other side of the mountain where there is no beach. Only steep cliffside. Since there is no danger of the merfolk entering from there, I requested that the witches leave that area open so that we dragons could come and go as we please."

I breathed out.

With that, the four men swept across the entrance hall and entered the tunnel leading toward the exit. I hurried after them as they reached the main door and barged outside into the clearing. As I emerged soon after, they were already starting their magnificent transformation. Their humanoid forms morphed and swelled in size until I was gazing up at four breathtakingly fierce beasts. Jeriad—with gorgeous silver-orange scales—reached a massive hand down for me. I tentatively gripped hold of his huge scaly fingers and stood in his palm. He raised me up onto his back. I positioned my legs either side of his thick neck and I barely had time to gain a hold on his scales before he launched upward into the sky, followed quickly by the others.

As we rose higher and higher, I held on for dear life. Soon we were level with the highest peaks of the mountains. We traveled over the range and, with the dragons' supernatural speed, soon reached the other side, where the ocean met the steep cliffside Jeriad had spoken of. As we flew over water, even despite Jeriad's assurances, I half expected the dragons to hit a solid barrier. Instead, we soared over the waves and headed toward the outermost boundary of The Shade.

I cast my eyes downward even as I focused on maintaining my grip—my palms had become sweaty from both the dragons' heat and my nerves. Holding on wasn't as easy as it should have been.

Now that I was scanning the surface of the ocean, I realized that there was more than just a single cluster of rocks near this island. I wasn't sure which one Ben had been referring to. We just had to keep searching.

As we flew, I explained what was happening and what had happened, but as we moved closer in line with the Port, my voice faltered. I caught sight of a scene that chilled me to the bone. We had found the right cluster.

Chapter 24: Sofia

As the sound of the motor neared, Jeramiah cast a lingering glance over the three of us.

"It's time for me to step out now," he said, moving backward. "But I'll stay nearby for a while to make sure things go smoothly…"

He turned to the witch and nodded. She planted a hand on his shoulder, and the two of them vanished.

Even while the vessel sounded like it was less than twenty feet away, I couldn't help but wish that Jeramiah had left his parasol behind for my father and me. Our limbs were still rigid as ever, and the sun beat mercilessly down upon us from the cloudless sky.

I couldn't see what state I was in—which was probably a good thing. Though as Derek, lying next to me, looked at me with worry, I sensed that my skin had begun to melt and peel. I was in more than enough agony for it. I didn't know how many minutes or hours we had been lying here in total, but I was reaching the limit of my pain tolerance—which, through unwilling training over the years, was at a much higher level than most vampires'.

After all my father had just been through, this was the last thing he needed. He was suffering enough mentally to not be subjected to this kind of physical pain. My blood boiled at the thought of what Jeramiah had done to him. Like Derek, I had also held out hope that, if we ever managed to meet Jeramiah, he would be different. That he wouldn't continue his father's—and grandfather's—legacy of malice and cruelty. Now it seemed that I'd hoped for too much. Far too much.

My thoughts froze as the growl of the engine died. Footsteps pounded over the rocks. Ten men came into view. They were dressed in black combat uniforms, their eyes obscured by dark shades. Clutched in their hands were shiny silver guns.

I looked desperately at Derek and then at my father, but we were as helpless as each other. The men closed the final distance between us and swooped down, gripping our limbs and hauling us over the sharp rocks. They dragged us to a boulder and propped us in an upright position.

The tallest hunter among them—and also the most slender in build—stepped forward. His eyes roamed the three of us.

"Derek and Sofia Novak, and Aiden Claremont, of The Shade. Is that correct?"

"You're barking up the wrong tree with us," I croaked. "Nobody on our island is a threat to you or any human."

His angular jaw set firmly. "We have some doubts about that," he said.

Swiveling to face Derek, he raised his gun and cocked it.

"No!" I rasped.

What followed happened almost too fast for my brain to process.

A mighty roar boomed down from the sky, so loud and fierce it made my hair stand on end.

The hunters froze and whirled around. Four magnificent dragons—Jeriad, Azaiah, Neros and Ridan, if I recognized them correctly in their beastly forms—soared toward us. Jeriad—who was leading the horde—widened his jaw and released a storm of flames. Fire blanketed the center of the islet, billowing dangerously close to us. The heat dried out my eyeballs and scorched my already fried skin.

Azaiah, Neros and Ridan joined Jeriad in releasing more fire, and soon I couldn't even see the hunters through the blaze. I did hear their gunshots, shouts, racing footsteps, and splashes of water as they no doubt retreated for safety. As the flames began to lick but a few meters away from our feet, I feared that they would consume us before the dragons came for us.

But then Ridan and Neros burst through the wall of smoke and fire. Ridan arrived at my side first. His massive left hand closed around my body as he lifted me up while his right hand reached for Derek. Neros picked up my father before the two dragons' wings beat heavily, raising us into the air. I was relieved that Ridan kept me lower against his body, beneath the shade of his broad chest. It felt like if my skin was tortured much more, it might become irreparably damaged.

Another round of lethal gunshots fired—one so unnervingly close, I heard it whoosh right past my ear. With all the smoke and flames, I could only just make out the outlines of Jeriad and Azaiah beneath us. My vision being hazy from all that forced sunlight didn't help either.

"The eyes, Amaya!" Jeramiah bellowed from somewhere beneath us.

Oh, no.

"Hurry!" I panicked.

We had to get to the boundary before the witch reached us.

Through the myriad of chaotic sounds broke out a thundering splash. I caught sight of Jeriad's giant tail thrashing in the water, while the rest of his body was submerged. He was clearly in agony.

"The witch must have gotten to his eyes," Derek shouted.

At this, Neros flew up to Ridan and transferred Aiden into Ridan's hand—the same hand that held me, for there was plenty of room for the two of us.

"I'm going down to assist," he said, doing a one-eighty and darting back down toward Jeriad.

Ridan continued hurtling forward with us toward the island and as he did, he began spouting fire all around us—I guessed to prevent the invisible witch coming too close. I thanked the heavens that we weren't far from the boundary and we managed to fly through it before Ridan got stabbed in the eye.

Although we were engulfed again by the darkness of The Shade, my skin was still singed. I cast a glance at Derek. His eyes were still fixed on the scene we'd just left. I gazed there too, even as I tried to calm my palpitating heart.

I could make out the hunters' speedboat dashing away now. Clearly they'd realized they weren't equipped to battle four angry dragons. Both Neros and Azaiah were hovering near the waves where Jeriad had fallen. I guessed the injured dragon would shift back into his humanoid form for his two companions to easily carry back to the island.

I wasn't sure how the dragons had known to come, but we

had just managed a narrow escape. I shuddered to think what would've happened had they arrived even a few moments later. I was certain that those hunters were going to take all of our lives, even as we'd informed them of our innocence.

The view of the ocean became obstructed as Ridan dipped behind a row of trees and touched down in a clearing near the Port.

Derek and I locked eyes, almost certain that the same questions were running through both of our heads. *What is up with these hunters?* They were so interested in stalking our island—they'd had naval ships stationed near our shores for months now, and they'd even tried to detect our every moment with motion sensors—yet now that they'd had three specimens from The Shade—including the king and queen at that—they'd simply wanted to kill us? If anything, they should have imprisoned us and taken us in for interrogation. The motives of the hunters were a complete mystery to me. *What exactly is their game?*

Our disturbed nephew, Jeramiah, was yet another enigma. I still wasn't sure how he'd entered the island, or what exactly he'd thought he would gain by traumatizing and murdering his family members. Revenge? Was that really all that drove him? I guessed it shouldn't have been surprising. Lust for vengeance had a way of blinding people to what was in front of them.

However jumbled my pain-ridden brain was with doubts and questions about the hunters and my nephew, as Ridan lowered us onto the lawn, there was one feeling of certainty that I couldn't shake: this wasn't the last time we'd cross paths with either of them.

Chapter 25: Ben

As I followed River riding atop Jeriad, away from the Black Heights and out of the boundary, I had a bad feeling about River accompanying the dragons. I wished that she could have stayed behind and let the dragons go by themselves. Then, when Amaya caught Jeriad's eyes with a curse, my fears came to fruition. Through the chaos and commotion, nobody noticed River slip from the dragon's back and crash into the waves.

I was afraid that she'd fallen too close to the jagged rocks, that she might have been injured by the force of her fall—half-bloods weren't as sturdy as vampires. I didn't know exactly how much they could endure. But then she emerged beneath a sky of fire.

"River!" I yelled.

Bolting through the smoke, flames, and even a couple of hunters as they aimed their bullets at the dragons, I leapt off the rocks. I glided over the surface of the ocean and reached River. As the waves rolled over her, she opened her mouth to shout, but the thick cloud of smoke stifled her. Disorientated, she was carried backward by the tide, which, to my horror, started swelling closer and closer to the hunters' speedboat.

She was strong. I didn't understand why she didn't kick her legs furiously and distance herself from it, but then I realized that she couldn't see the speedboat. I could see in this smog, but the dragons' offense was blinding her, and by the time she realized where she was headed, it was too late. She brushed up against the side of the speedboat and one of the men noticed her. His arms shot down and grabbed her by the shoulders. Before she could even react, he'd yanked her up over the edge of the boat.

"No!" I roared, my voice sounding on par with the dragons' bellows as it echoed in my head.

I leapt onto the boat after her. Six hunters were now bent over her, grabbing her limbs as she kicked and thrashed. Then one pulled out a gun and jammed it against her temple, forcing her into submission. I feared that they were going to treat her the same as my parents—that the hunter was seconds away from pulling the trigger—but instead, they fastened metal restraints around her wrists and arms. Then they dragged her through an open hatch. I sped through to find that it led down to a small, lower deck.

She struggled against her restraints, but they must have been strong. For all her supernatural strength, she couldn't break through them.

As they carried her to a wide bench in one corner, a man yelled from above deck, "Let's go! Let's go!" The engine roared, and the speedboat lurched.

The men backed away from River, though four remained watching her, guns still ready in their hands. A pain lanced my chest as River begged, "Please, let me go." She was soaked to the bone, and it killed me to see how much she was shivering.

I glared around at the hunters, trying to see if I could recognize any of them. Most had removed their shades, but I couldn't. None of these men bore burns, so I guessed that they had remained on the boat. Despite just witnessing an attack of gigantic, fire-breathing dragons, all looked quite calm, as though they saw this kind of thing every day.

What do they want with River?

Back near The Oasis, after we had first escaped and ventured out into the desert—a desert that was closely guarded by hunters—I remembered how she had almost died from one of the bullets. They'd chosen to attack without even hearing her out, so I expected them to behave in the same way here. Plunge a bullet into her chest or skull. But they didn't.

The speed the boat was traveling at unnerved me. When it began to slow, I left River temporarily to poke my head out through the hatch. We had arrived near the huge naval ships. I expected us to head right for one of them, where they'd likely carry River aboard, but instead they stopped two dozen feet away from it.

"Doug, are you ready with the sub?" A man near the bow—the same tall, wiry man who'd addressed my parents on the rocks—spoke into an earpiece.

A few moments later, a submarine surfaced in front of us. It poked out from beneath the waves and a hatch lifted open.

The tall man nodded to another hunter, who descended to the lower deck and instructed the men watching over River to carry her up. They grabbed her and hoisted her over their heads as they transferred her from the speedboat to the submarine. Even bound and with all four men, each of them about twice her size, manhandling her, she still managed to make it difficult for them. But not difficult enough. She was shoved down through the submarine's hatch, and as I followed, four more men were waiting for her. They picked her up and carried her along a narrow corridor.

"Let me go! Please!" River's voice cut me again.

It's my fault she's here.

They ignored her completely. They reached the end of the corridor and stopped outside a cabin. One of the men reached for a chain of keys from his back pocket and opened the door, one-handed. They moved her into the room—a small, bare room whose walls were made of some kind of grey metal, with a bed, a trashcan, and a tiny bathroom. They planted her down on the bed and then exited.

The submarine shuddered and jolted downward. We were submerging. Away from the naval ships. Away from The Shade.

Where are they taking her?

I gazed down at River. They hadn't even bothered to untie her. She just lay there uncomfortably on the mattress. "Let me go!" she yelled, her voice hoarse and cracked. "Please!"

I knelt on the floor so that my face was level with hers as she squirmed on the bed. I reached out and traced her face with my hand, wishing more than I ever had before that she could feel my touch. That I could offer her even the slightest reassurance.

If I'd still been a vampire, I would have flung her over my shoulder, torn down the door and ripped through as many hunters' throats as I needed to get River out of here—or died trying.

But here I knelt, unable to even reach out and touch my

girl, let alone fight for her.

I stared down at my pale, translucent hands.

That vial of potion may have given me life... But what kind of life is this?

Epilogue: Aisha

I was still stuck in the box.

I didn't know how much time had passed since Ben had gotten pulled out, but I had long passed the brink of desperation. I was too exhausted to shed more tears. After the vampire left, I'd spent every moment crushed with the worry of what had happened to him and what was happening to my family back in The Oasis.

To make matters worse, the ship had been motionless for what felt like days. I could only assume that Julie and her crew had abandoned it, left it drifting somewhere in the ocean. I'd begun to believe that I would never get out. I just sat curled up in a corner, trying to numb my mind. It was the least painful state of existence that I could find for myself.

Then one day—or perhaps it was during the night; I had no way of knowing—the ship jolted to a start. I scrambled upright, my eyes wide, ears perked. The vessel hadn't been abandoned after all and the thought brought me a sliver of hope in the gloom.

Minutes passed, and the ship only seemed to be gaining speed.

I was jerked against the side of the box by something heavy crashing against it. My head banged painfully against the wall. It sounded like a weight had fallen upon the lid of the box. I stared upward at the inside of the lid, my eyes wide with anticipation, barely daring to breathe. Then I heard a sound that made my heart skip a beat.

The clinking of a key. The scraping of metal against a lock. A click.

I must have been dreaming. Even as the lid began to lift open, my brain still hadn't accepted that this was actually happening. The box was opening. *Oh, gods of all things good.*

I gathered myself together, preparing to spring out when a heavy, damp, furry body was flung inside the box and crashed on top of me. I hadn't yet transformed myself into my subtle state, and the weight toppled me and crushed me beneath it. I quickly dissolved my body, allowing me to slide out from underneath it with ease.

Rising up, I found myself staring down at a dead werewolf. It had been gouged in the throat. The fur around its neck was drenched in blood, and there were deep wounds in the flesh around its throat. My eyes darted upward, toward the opening of the box, and I zoomed out…

I'm free. I'm free!

The euphoria surging through my spirit temporarily drove any wondering from my mind about who had opened the box and dropped that corpse inside.

I had emerged in a small room, some kind of storage room. Clearly at the base of the ship. My eyes lowered to the floor. Drops of blood trailed from the box to the door. It must've been caused by dragging that werewolf in here… *Who was that?*

I glanced at a set of keys lying on the floor, unceremoniously discarded as soon as the box was opened and the wolf dumped inside.

I moved to the exit and floated out into a dim corridor. I was surprised by the state of the place. Julie's ship looked an absolute wreck. More bloodstains coated the dusty floors, there were shreds of what looked like old curtains and carpets scattered about and the walls looked like they'd been clawed by wild animals. It was like a ghoul had been let loose to rip through the ship.

Noises came from the deck above. I left the deserted corridor and moved up the stairs. Pushing open the trap door and emerging out in the open—into a dark, cloudy night—I almost swallowed my tongue.

Surrounding me was a scene of utter horror. Piled on the long deck were row upon row of… vampires? They all lay on their backs, tossing and turning and writhing in agony. Each had puncture marks in their necks, their heads resting in pools of their own blood.

Floorboards creaked behind me. I whirled around to find myself face to face with… I didn't even know what they were. They looked like creatures who belonged in a nightmare. They stood, rawboned and naked, with stark-white papery skin and bald skulls. Their faces were gaunt, with slightly receded noses and small black dots for eyes. There must have been at least sixty of them.

I was still on Julie's ship, wasn't I?

What the hell happened here?

My heart pounded as one of them jolted toward me, its reedy arms outstretched. Long black claws extended from its fingers and it bared fangs… fangs that reminded me of a vampire's, except longer, sharper, more protruding. I shot upward to dodge the creature's advance and hovered near the sails as I gazed down at the horrific scene.

I glanced out toward the ocean to spot in the distance an

island. It looked like The Tavern. The vessel was speeding away—The Tavern must have been where the ship had stopped— and following us were three other ships. A loud explosion blasted from one of them, and a giant canon ball hurtled toward the bow of Julie's ship. It narrowly missed, but was soon followed by half a dozen more explosions. Heavy metal ball after ball came thundering toward the ship— most grazing it, while a couple even penetrated the vessel's body.

But what are these creatures who have overtaken Julie's ship? And what's happening to those vampires writhing on the ground? It looked like they were... turning. But they were already vampires. Weren't they?

Whatever these creatures were, it appeared that they'd done something to anger the people of the Tavern. Julie's sharks however, seemed to be far stronger and faster than any of the ships chasing after us. The ship endured another shower of cannon balls, but then the sharks managed to create more distance between us and the attackers and they could no longer reach us. Then it seemed that the aggressors slowed and gave up altogether.

As my eyes drifted over the rows of squirming vampires, my blood ran cold. One of them appeared to be thrashing about in particular pain. He looked different than the others, too—his skin much whiter and his body emaciated.

He reached a hand up into his mop of thick brown hair and, closing his fist around it, began to tug violently. A clump pulled away in his hand. He dropped it to the floor and then slid both hands against his skull to draw out two more clumps. By the fifth pull, the hair seemed to be coming out much more easily—he barely even needed to tug. Just running his fingers against his scalp seemed to cause masses to shed... until he had not even a single strand left.

Rolling over on his stomach, he gathered himself together and stood up shakily to his full height. His gaunt face contorted, he teetered on his feet and began tearing the clothes from his body as though they were on fire. Then his eyes set forward and fixed on the frightful creatures standing in a pack on the other side of the deck.

The one who'd motioned to attack me loped forward and grabbed the hand of the sickly vampire, pulling him over to join the rest of its wraithlike comrades. It was as the vampire stood next to the creature, and I gazed at their faces side by side—growing more eerily alike by the moment—that the chilling realization crashed down upon me like a bucket of ice shards.

I couldn't believe the sight, and yet I knew that I was not hallucinating.

Taking place before my very eyes was a phenomenon that I

was certain had never occurred before in all of supernatural history.

God forbid… Could this really be happening?

What's next?

Dear Shaddict,

Here are two exciting new releases to mark in your calendar:

1st Release:
A SHADE OF DRAGON CONTINUED!

Get your next dose of Nell and Theon in *A Shade of Dragon 2*, releasing January 6th 2016. The penultimate book in the trilogy!

Visit **www.bellaforrest.net** for details on ordering your copy now.

Here's a preview of the cover:

2nd Release:
BEN & RIVER'S STORY CONTINUED!

Prepare for the next part of Ben and River's story: *A Shade of Vampire 22: A Fork of Paths*!

A Fork of Paths releases January 22nd 2016.

Again, visit: **www.bellaforrest.net** for details on ordering.

And here's a preview of the cover:

Thank you for reading.

Love,

Bella x

P.S. Join my VIP email list and I'll send you a personal reminder as soon as I have a new book out. Visit here to sign up: www.forrestbooks.com

(You'll also be the first to receive news about movies/TV show as well as other exciting projects coming up!)

P.P.S. Follow The Shade on Instagram and check out some of the beautiful graphics: @ashadeofvampire

You can also come say hi to me on Facebook: www.facebook.com/AShadeOfVampire

And Twitter: @ashadeofvampire

I'd love to hear from you.

Made in the USA
San Bernardino, CA
26 December 2015